SAMUEL
FRENCH

FOUNDED 1830

New York Hollywood London Toronto

SAMUELFRENCH.COM

*see p. 5.

OPENING NIGHT JANUARY 5, 1975

MAJESTIC THEATRE

KEN HARPER
presents

THE WIZ

The new musical version of
The Wonderful Wizard of Oz
(L. Frank Baum)

Book by
WILLIAM F. BROWN

Music and Lyrics by
CHARLIE SMALLS

starring

TIGER HAYNES

TED ROSS

HINTON BATTLE

CLARICE TAYLOR

MABEL KING

ANDRE DE SHIELDS **TASHA THOMAS** **DEE DEE BRIDGEWATER**
(Is The Wiz)

also starring

STEPHANIE MILLS as Dorothy

Setting Designed by
TOM H. JOHN

Costumes Designed by
GEOFFREY HOLDER

Lighting Designed by
THARON MUSSER

Orchestrations by
HAROLD WHEELER

Musical Direction
and Vocal Arrangements by
CHARLES H. COLEMAN

Dance Arrangements by
TIMOTHY GRAPHENREED

Choreography and Musical Numbers Staged by
GEORGE FAISON

Directed by
GEOFFREY HOLDER

An orchestration consisting of:

    2 Piano/conductor scores (includes synthesizer cues)
    Reed I (flute, alto sax)
    Reed II (flute, alto sax)
    Reed III (alto flute, clarinet, tenor sax)
    Reed IV (oboe, baritone sax)
    Trumpet I & II
    Trumpet III
    Horn
    Trombone I
    Trombone II
    Percussion (inc. timpani, bells, vibraphone, xylophone)
      (2 books)
    Drums
    Violins (2 books)
    Cello
    Bass
    Guitar

    20 chorus books

will be loaned two months prior to the production ONLY on
receipt of the royalty quoted for all performances, the rental fee
and a refundable deposit. The deposit will be refunded on the
safe return to SAMUEL FRENCH, INC. of all materials loaned
for the production.

Vocal Selections: $12.95, plus postage

CAST
(In Order of Appearance)

AUNT EM .... *Tasha Thomas*
TOTO .... *Nancy*
DOROTHY .... *Stephanie Mills*
UNCLE HENRY .... *Ralph Wilcox*
TORNADO .... *Evelyn Thomas*
MUNCHKINS .... *Phylicia Ayers-Allen, Pi Douglass,*
Joni Palmer, Andy Torres, Carl Weaver
ADDAPERLE .... *Clarice Taylor*
YELLOW BRICK ROAD .... *Ronald Dunham, Eugene Little,*
John Parks, Kenneth Scott
SCARECROW .... *Hinton Battle*
CROWS .... *Wendy Edmead, Frances Morgan, Ralph Wilcox*
TINMAN .... *Tiger Haynes*
LION .... *Ted Ross*
KALIDAHS .... *Phillip Bond, Pi Douglass, Rodney Green,*
Evelyn Thomas, Andy Torres
POPPIES .... *Lettie Battle, Leslie Butler, Eleanor McCoy,*
Frances Morgan, Joni Palmer
FIELD MICE .... *Phylicia Ayers-Allen, Pi Douglass,*
Carl Weaver, Ralph Wilcox
GATEKEEPER .... *Danny Beard*
EMERALD CITY CITIZENS .... *Lettie Battle, Leslie Butler,*
Wendy Edmead, Eleanor McCoy, Frances Morgan,
Joni Palmer, Evelyn Thomas, Philip Bond,
Ronald Dunham, Rodney Green,
Eugene Little, John Parks, Kenneth Scott, Andy Torres
THE WIZ .... *Andre De Shields*
EVILLENE .... *Mabel King*
LORD HIGH UNDERLING .... *Ralph Wilcox*
SOLDIER MESSENGER .... *Carl Weaver*
WINGED MONKEY .... *Andy Torres*
GLINDA .... *Dee Dee Bridgewater*

SCENES AND MUSICAL NUMBERS

ACT ONE

PROLOGUE—KANSAS
"The Feeling We Once Had" .... *Aunt Em*
"Tornado Ballet" .... *Company*
SCENE 1—MUNCHKIN LAND
"He's The Wiz" .... *Addaperle, Munchkins*
SCENE 2—OZ COUNTRYSIDE
"Soon As I Get Home" .... *Dorothy*
"I Was Born on the Day Before Yesterday" .... *Scarecrow, Crows*
"Ease On Down the Road" .... *Dorothy, Scarecrow, Yellow Brick Road*
SCENE 3—WOODS
"Slide Some Oil To Me" .... *Tinman, Dorothy, Scarecrow*
"Ease on Down the Road" (reprise) .... *Dorothy, Scarecrow,*
Tinman, Yellow Brick Road
SCENE 4—JUNGLE
"Mean Ole Lion" .... *Lion*
"Ease on Down the Road" (reprise) .... *Dorothy, Scarecrow, Tinman,*
Lion, Yellow Brick Road
SCENE 5—KALIDAH COUNTRY
"Kalidah Battle" .... *Friends, Kalidahs, Yellow Brick Road*
SCENE 6—POPPY FIELD
"Be A Lion" .... *Dorothy, Lion*
"Lion's Dream" .... *Lion, Poppies*
SCENE 7—EMERALD CITY
"Emerald City Ballet (Pssst)" .... *Friends, Company*
Music by Timothy Graphenreed and George Faison
SCENE 8—THRONE ROOM
"So You Wanted To Meet The Wizard" .... *The Wiz*
"To Be Able To Feel" .... *Tinman*

ACT TWO

SCENE 1—WEST WITCH CASTLE
"No Bad News" .... *Evillene*
SCENE 2—FOREST
"Funky Monkeys" .... *Monkeys*
SCENE 3—COURTYARD
"Everybody Rejoice" .... *Friends, Winkies*
Music and Lyrics by Luther Vandross
SCENE 4—EMERALD CITY GATE
SCENE 5—THRONE ROOM
"Who Do You Think You Are?" .... *Friends*
"Believe In Yourself" .... *The Wiz*
SCENE 6—FAIRGROUNDS
"Y'all Got It!" .... *The Wiz*
SCENE 7—OUTSKIRTS
SCENE 8—QUADLING COUNTRY
"A Rested Body is a Rested Mind" .... *Glinda*
"Believe In Yourself" (rep.) .... *Glinda*
"Home" .... *Dorothy*

The Wiz

PROLOGUE

Overture.

S.R., *we see a small, rather ramshackle little farm house in Kansas.* U.S. *there is a clothesline, and* AUNT EM *is unpinning various items of clothing. She keeps an eye on the dark and brooding sky as she drops the clothes in a basket. Both* AUNT EM *and* UNCLE HENRY *are in their late thirties, perhaps, but life has not been easy for them so far, and promises little else.*

A small mongrel dog, TOTO, *runs across from* S.L. *to* S.R., *barking playfully.* AUNT EM *gives the dog a glance and shakes her head. Closely behind the dog comes a girl of thirteen or fourteen, dressed in her best Sunday dress. Her name is* DOROTHY, *and she's as bright and alive as can be. Somehow, it would seem she's built a life of her own on this dreary farm, and would probably rather remain a child as long as possible instead of accepting the responsibilities of adulthood.*

DOROTHY. (*Running on from* D.L. *to* D.R.) Toto! Toto, you come back here!

AUNT EM. (*About to ask for help with the wash.*) Dorothy . . .

DOROTHY. Toto! You hear me?

AUNT EM. (*A little more sharply.*) Dorothy, I been needin' help all afternoon!

DOROTHY. (*Crossing to* R. *of* AUNT EM.) Soon as I get Toto, Aunt Em. (*She spies him* O.S.) Toto! (*Runs Off* R., *above porch.* AUNT EM *rolls her eyes as* UNCLE HENRY *crosses behind her.*)

UNCLE HENRY. (*Entering from* L-2.) You an' Dorothy at it again, Emily?

AUNT EM. Lord, I don't *believe* that child!

UNCLE HENRY. (*He exits as* DOROTHY *returns with* TOTO. *As he crosses above her.*) You'd better hurry up, a big storm is heading this way. (*Exits* R-2.)

DOROTHY. (*Entering* D.S.R. *with* TOTO.) Now what was it you wanted me to do?

AUNT EM. (*Picks up basket of laundry.*) I did it *m'self!*

DOROTHY. (*Crosses to* L. *of* C.) Oh.

AUNT EM. (*Testy; crossing to below storm cellar.*) I wanted a hand with these here clothes before the storm blew 'em all away!

DOROTHY. I'm sorry, Aunt Em. I didn't . . .

AUNT EM. (*Stops.* UNCLE HENRY *enters* U.S. *house, looks, exits* L-2.) . . . *think.* No, you never do, child. Now we're fixin' for a twister an' you're playin' (DOROTHY *sits* C.) games with that dog. And in your Sunday dress, too! (*Putting basket just* R. *of storm cellar doors.*) Serve you right if you *both* blew away!

DOROTHY. (*Still seated on ground,* L. *of* C.) I imagine it would.

AUNT EM (*Turning to her.*) What was that?

DOROTHY. Aw, I'm not much help around here for you and Uncle Henry. Always daydreaming and stuff. I bet it would be a big load off your back if I did blow away, wouldn't it?

AUNT EM. (*After a moment of seriousness, puts* DOROTHY *on.*) I imagine it would.

MUSIC #2: *"THE FEELING WE ONCE HAD"*

DOROTHY. (*Hurt.*) It would?

AUNT EM. Dorothy . . . you know how much your Uncle Henry and I love you, don't you? (*On the line, she moves* S.L. *to* DOROTHY, *up of her and to* DOROTHY'*s left.*)

PUT YOUR ARMS AROUND ME, CHILD
LIKE WHEN YOU BUMPED YOUR SHIN
THEN YOU'LL KNOW I LOVE YOU NOW
AS I LOVED YOU THEN
    (*Kneels, right knee down.*)

THOUGH YOU MAY BE TRYING SOMETIMES
AND I'LL NEED YOU AND YOU'RE NOT THERE
    (*Turns* DOROTHY'*s face to her.*)
I MAY GET MAD AND TURN YOU AWAY
    (*Puts* DOROTHY'*s head on her shoulder.*)
BUT I STILL CARE.
    (DOROTHY *puts head down on* AUNT EM'*s left thigh.*)

BUT YOU SHOULDN'T ASK FOR MORE
THAN CAN COME FROM ME
    (AUNT EM *gets* DOROTHY'*s eye contact.*)

I AM DIFFERENT THAN YOU ARE,
AND ONE DAY YOU'LL SEE
    (*Open front. Eye contact.*)

IF I LOSE MY PATIENCE WITH YOU
AND I SUDDENLY START TO SCREAM
IT'S ONLY BECAUSE I WANT YOU TO BE
    (*Open toward* S.L.)
WHAT I SEE IN MY DREAMS.
    (*Move close.*)

AND I'D LIKE TO KNOW THAT IT'S THERE
THE FEELING WE ONCE HAD
    (*Touch* DOROTHY's *face.*)
KNOWING THAT YOU CAN COME TO ME
WHENEVER YOU'RE FEELING SAD.

    PIT SINGERS.
DON'T LOSE THE FEELING WE ONCE HAD
DON'T LOSE THE FEELING WE ONCE HAD
    (AUNT EM *rise during* PIT SINGERS' *phrase.*)

    AUNT EM. (*Helps* DOROTHY *up.*)
THOUGH YOU ARE GROWING OLDER NOW
AND I'M WATCHING YOU GROW
    (DOROTHY *turns away a bit embarrassed.*)
AND IF I MAKE YOU SAD SOMETIMES
    (DOROTHY *goes to her for embrace.*)
I SEE YOUR FEELINGS SHOW
    (*Both cross to* R.C.)

AND ONE DAY I'LL LOOK AROUND
AND YOU WILL BE GROWN
    (AUNT EM *pushes* DOROTHY *toward* S.R.)
YOU'LL BE OUT IN THE WORLD
    (AUNT EM *curtseys.*)
SUCH A PRETTY LITTLE GIRL
    (DOROTHY *curtseys.*)
BUT YOU'LL BE ON YOUR OWN
    (DOROTHY, *frightened at the prospect, runs to* AUNT EM *for embrace.*)

AND I'D LIKE TO KNOW THAT IT'S THERE
THE FEELING WE ONCE HAD
    (*At arms length.*)
KNOWING THAT YOU CAN COME TO ME
WHENEVER YOU'RE FEELING BAD
THE FEELING WE ONCE HAD
    (*Open to hold both hands.*)
THE FEELING WE ONCE HAD
DON'T LOSE THE FEELING
THE FEELING WE ONCE HAD.
    (*Embrace.*)

UNCLE HENRY. (*Enters on the run, picks up the milk can from* D.L.C. *and continues toward* D.R.) Em! Dorothy! Hurry! This here's a big one! (UNCLE HENRY *puts milk can behind barrel on the house platform,* L. *of cellar door. They struggle to get into the cellar.*)

MUSIC #3: *TORNADO BALLET*

(*The following dialogue and pit ensemble dialogue takes place during the TORNADO BALLET.*)

DOROTHY. Aunt Em.
PITS. I'm comin' to getcha.
Gotcha, Gotcha.
Getcha . . . comin' to
Getcha.
Getcha . . . comin' to
Getcha.
Oooo.
Oooo.
Oooo.
Comin' to getcha.
Comin' to getcha.
Gotcha.
Gotcha.
Gotcha.

        (*BLACKOUT, except silhouette.*)

MUSIC #3A: *MUNCHKINS' ENTRANCE*

ACT ONE

SCENE 1

The Land of the Munchkins. Some time later.

*The porch has come to rest in a strange land, full of strange shapes,
and with a strange sun in the sky. As the lights slowly come up,*
DOROTHY *is still on the porch, which has spun through the
tornado, and has come to rest just left of* C.S.

Two wall sections have come on from R-2, *and* ADDAPERLE'S *tent
has come on from* L-2.

Two MUNCHKINS *enter from* L-1, *and a third from* R-1. *They
approach the wreckage cautiously.*

DOROTHY. (*On porch.*) Aunt Em! Aunt Em! Where are you? Aunt
Em! *Aunt Em!*
    FIRST MUNCHKIN. (*Crossing to* D.L. *of* C.) Aunt Em?
    THIRD MUNCHKIN. (*At* S.R. *of porch.*) Aunt Em?
    SECOND MUNCHKIN. (D.S. *of Tent unit.*) Aunt Em?
    DOROTHY. (*Now she sees the strange little people, and draws
back in fear.*) You're not Aunt Em!
    THIRD MUNCHKIN. (*Crossing to and asking* FIRST MUNCHKIN.)
Who's Aunt Em?
    DOROTHY. (*Crossing* D.S. *off porch.*) Where am I?
    FIRST MUNCHKIN. (*Crossing* D.S., *and then a bit* S.L., SECOND
MUNCHKIN *counter* U.S.) In the Land of Oz, where the Munchkins
live.
    THIRD MUNCHKIN. (*Crossing* S.L. *and surveying the damage of
the porch, discovers a pair of feet sticking out from under the porch.
They wear the silver slippers of* EVVAMENE, THE WICKED WITCH OF
THE EAST, *and loud red and white striped panty hose.*) Ahhh!
(*Moves* D.S. *of the other two, and to* D.L.) Look! She done set that
house on Evvamene!
    FIRST MUNCHKIN. (*Crossing* U.S. *to look for herself.*) Is she dead?
    SECOND MUNCHKIN. (*Said to* THIRD MUNCHKIN . . . *she is be-
tween* FIRST *and* THIRD.) Yeah, and I don't think she's gonna like it!

(DOROTHY *now also sees legs, and backs to* S.R. *of the house, unaware of what the consequences will be.*)

FIRST MUNCHKIN. (*Crossing to* DOROTHY, *hand extended.*) Congratulations! (*Crossing* D.S. *of* DOROTHY *to her right.*)

SECOND MUNCHKIN. (*Crossing to the left of* DOROTHY.) You just killed The Wicked Witch of the East.

DOROTHY. (*Crossing* D.S. *of* SECOND MUNCHKIN *to* L.C.) Oh, no!

THIRD MUNCHKIN. (*From* D.L., *crosses* U.S. *of* DOROTHY *and to her right.*) Oh, yeah!

FIRST MUNCHKIN. Girl, I'm gonna wear *white* to the funeral. (*Does hand slap with* SECOND MUNCHKIN.)

DOROTHY. (*Terrified, runs from them toward* S.L., *and when* D.S. *of the tent unit* . . .) I didn't mean to kill nobody!

MUSIC #4:   *ADDAPERLE'S ENTRANCE*

(*The center section of the tent flies out, revealing a huge cloud of* CO_2 *smoke, and as it clears, we see* ADDAPERLE, THE GOOD WITCH OF THE NORTH, *sputtering, and spitting. At the sound of the tent opening,* DOROTHY *and all three* MUNCHKINS *have scattered toward* S.R., *with* DOROTHY *the furthest* O.S.)

ADDAPERLE. What's goin' on around here!

MUNCHKINS. Addaperle! (*They all move toward her.*)

THIRD MUNCHKIN. (*Getting to her first, circling* D.S. *and to her left.*) Let me have your autograph, girl. (ADDAPERLE *favors each of them with finger-kiss autographs, and upon receiving them, they also move* D.S. *and to her left.*)

DOROTHY. (*Still* S.R., *wide-eyed.*) Who are you?

ADDAPERLE. The Good Witch of the North.

DOROTHY. The Good Witch of the North?

ADDAPERLE. (*Crossing to* R. *of* C.) Maybe you know me better by my stage name . . . Addaperle, the Feelgood Girl!

(*The* MUNCHKINS *clap eight times.*)

DOROTHY. (*Crosses in toward her.*) Your *stage* name?

ADDAPERLE. Yes, I have a magic act. (*She whips a small collapsible bouquet of paper flowers out of her waist band* . . .) I do tricks! (*On the word "tricks," she pops the bouquet open.*)

(MUNCHKIN #FOUR *and* FIVE *now enter from* U.S. *of the tent unit, and circling above the porch and to the* S.R. *side of it, spy* EVVAMENE'S *legs sticking out.*)

THIRD MUNCHKIN. (*Down and left of porch.*) Does she ever!

ADDAPERLE. (*Turning to him.*) You better cool it, or I'll turn you into something.

THIRD MUNCHKIN. (*Crossing to* S.L. *of* ADDAPERLE.) Addaperle, this child here, she done gone and set her house down on your sister, Evvamene.

ADDAPERLE. (*Crossing* D.S. *of him, and to the base of the feet.*) Ohhhh! (*Covers face, moment of grief . . . not too serious.*)

FIRST MUNCHKIN. That is old Evvamene, ain't it?

ADDAPERLE. (*Cries.*) Yes! (*Partial recovery.*) I'd know those tacky panty hose of hers anywhere! (*Total recovery . . . crossing* D.S.) That means there's only three witches left in Oz. Me, The Good Witch of the North. (*She laughs.* MUNCHKINS *fold hands and smile.*) My sister, Glinda, The Good Witch of the South . . . MUNCHKINS *big grin.*) You ought to see her act, honey. (MUNCH-KINS *nod. . .* ADDAPERLE *laughs.*) And then there's Evillene . . .

MUNCHKINS. Evillene!! (*They bless themselves two times, clasp hands, bow heads, most-holy.*)

ADDAPERLE. (*Blessing self . . . just in case.*) . . . The Wicked Witch of the West. You better watch out for her. She's a real downer. (MUNCHKINS *nod yes.* ADDAPERLE *crosses to* DOROTHY. MUNCHKIN #4 *crosses* U.S. *of* ADDAPERLE *and* DOROTHY *to* D.R.) Now, let's get down to business, honey. What's your name, child?

DOROTHY. Well, my name is . . .

ADDAPERLE. Wait! Don't tell me. I'll ask my magic slate.

(*She moves* U.S. *of* DOROTHY, *puts down her magic bag, and pulls out a small blackboard, with a piece of chalk attached. She hands slate to the* D.R. MUNCHKIN #4 *who holds it up for all to see.*)

DOROTHY. Your what?

ADDAPERLE. My magic slate. Now, I ain't gonna touch this slate . . . (*She crosses* U.S. *of* DOROTHY *to* C. . . . *going to do her act.*) but on it, the name of this child shall be written. (*Big preparation.*) And that name is . . . (*2 Orchestra Sounds.*) Shirley!!

DOROTHY. No.

ADDAPERLE. (*Still hanging in.*) Denise!!

DOROTHY. No.

ADDAPERLE. (*Starting to collapse.*) Starletta?

DOROTHY. (*Now amused at this lady.*) No.

ADDAPERLE. (*Starting to cross* U.S. *of* DOROTHY.) Urylee?

DOROTHY. No.

ADDAPERLE. (*Crosses back to over* DOROTHY'S *right shoulder.*)
Mary Bethune?

DOROTHY. No.

ADDAPERLE. (*Crossing to magic slate.*) Mitzi?

DOROTHY. No . . . My name is . . .

ADDAPERLE. (*Grabbing slate from* MUNCHKIN #4, *and handing it
to* DOROTHY, *a bit annoyed.*) Then *write* your name on this magic
slate. (*Then, turning to the* MUNCHKINS.) Well, you can't win 'em
all. (DOROTHY, *having written her name on the slate, hands it back
to* ADDAPERLE. ADDAPERLE, *smiling sweetly at* DOROTHY, *pushes
her face toward the* MUNCHKINS S.L., *and then pretends magic.*
DOROTHY *does a "What's going on?" look to the* MUNCHKINS, *who
cover their eyes with their fingers.*)
Ibbiddy, Dibbiddy, an' more of the same . . .
Now I'm beginning to see the name . . .

　　　(*Three chords from orchestra.*)
Dorothy!! (*At the name* DOROTHY, *the* MUNCHKINS *uncover their
eyes.*)

DOROTHY. You call that magic?

ADDAPERLE. Listen, child, I'm doing the best I can. (*Crosses to
her bag, returns slate.*)

DOROTHY. (*Tempo up, crosses below* ADDAPERLE *to* D.R.) Then
could you help me get home to Kansas? (MUNCHKIN #4 *places*
ADDAPERLE'S *magic bag on her own* S.R. *side. Crosses to* D.C.)
Kansas? Oh, I don't think so. That comes under the heading of
transporting a minor across state lines. (MUNCHKINS *all nod "Yes."*)
Maybe you better go see the Wiz!

MUSIC #5:   *"HE'S THE WIZ"*

(*On the vamp,* MUNCHKINS #4 & 5 *bring* DOROTHY *to* D.C.,
　　ADDAPERLE *moves to* DOROTHY'S S.R. *side to start number.*)

FIRST MUNCHKIN. Yeah! She'll have to go see the Wiz.

SECOND MUNCHKIN. I bet he could do it!

THIRD MUNCHKIN. Dorothy'll have to go see the Wiz!

DOROTHY. Who?

ADDAPERLE. (*And the* MUNCHKINS.)
SWEET THING, LET ME TELL YOU 'BOUT
THE WORLD AND THE WAY THINGS ARE—A
YOU'VE COME FROM A DIFFERENT PLACE

AND I KNOW YOU'VE TRAVELLED FAR—A
NOW THAT YOU'VE TOLD ME WHAT IT IS
    (MUNCHKINS *open out.*)
I'D BETTER POINT YOU TOWARD THE WIZ.
    (*All point* S.L.)
HE'S THE WIZ
HE'S THE ONE, HE'S THE ONLY ONE
WHO CAN GIVE YOUR WISH RIGHT TO YA
    —(HE'S THE WIZARD)
HE CAN SEND YOU BACK THROUGH TIME
BY RUNNIN' MAGIC THROUGH YA
ALL OF THE SUPER POWER'S HIS
LISTEN AND I'LL TELL YOU WHERE HE IS
HE'S THE WIZ AND HE LIVES IN OZ
    —(HE'S THE WIZARD)

THERE'S THE WAY TO THE EMERALD CITY
NOW THAT'S NOT TOO FAR, IS IT?
    —(HE'S THE WIZARD)
JUST TAKE YOUR DILEMMA, CHILD
AND LAY IT ON THE WIZARD
HE'LL FIX YOU A DRINK THAT'LL BUBBLE AND
    FOAM
    (*Crossing* S.R.)
AND IN A FLASH, YOU WILL BE HOME

HE'S THE WIZ
HE'S THE WIZARD OF OZ
HE'S GOT MAGIC UP HIS SLEEVE
    —(HE'S THE WIZARD)
AND YOU KNOW WITHOUT HIS HELP
'TWOULD BE IMPOSSIBLE TO LEAVE
FANTASTIC POWER AT HIS COMMAND
AND I'M SURE THAT HE WILL UNDERSTAND
HE'S THE WIZ
AND HE LIVES IN OZ
HE'S THE WIZARD—HE'S THE WIZARD
  DOROTHY.
HE'S THE WIZARD!!

(*As the number ends in tableau,* R. *of* C., DOROTHY *is on the* S.L. *side
of* ADDAPERLE.)

ADDAPERLE. (*Big hug with* DOROTHY.) But before you go, maybe you ought to take Evvamene's silver slippers. (MUNCHKINS *all pull back.* MUNCHKIN #4 *scurries* U.S. *and gets slippers off the feet sticking out from under the porch, and brings to* ADDAPERLE. ADDAPERLE, *putting shoes on* DOROTHY's *feet.*) Here. I hope you don't mind second-hand shoes.

DOROTHY. I never had a pair this beautiful.

ADDAPERLE. (*Blessing shoes.*) But, you gotta *promise* not to take them off till you get home!

DOROTHY. Alright, I promise . . . but why?

ADDAPERLE. (*Rising, with* DOROTHY's *shoes.*) 'Cause they really got some secret powers. (*The* MUNCHKINS *close in to hear.*)

DOROTHY. To do what?

ADDAPERLE. (*A step to* S.R., *and back.*) I don't know. That's the secret.

(ADDAPERLE *again starts to* S.R. *The* MUNCHKINS *break away disgusted.* ADDAPERLE *comes back with an afterthought through* . . .)

DOROTHY. Well, they're just my size, anyway.

ADDAPERLE. (*Returning to* DOROTHY.) And this kiss . . .(*Kisses* DOROTHY's *forehead.*)

MUNCHKINS. Aw!

(*Orchestra Chime.*)

ADDAPERLE. . . . will protect you wherever you go! (*Starts to go* S.R., *then another afterthought.*) Except in the poppy field! (MUNCHKINS *shake fingers "NO!"*)

DOROTHY. What's wrong with poppies?

ADDAPERLE. (*With* DOROTHY's *shoes, crossing to her magic bag* D.R.) Oh, this kind will put you to sleep for a hundred years. (MUNCHKINS *nod three times.*) It's terrible, wakin' up and your clothes are all outta style . . . (MUNCHKINS *nod four times.* ADDAPERLE *picks up her bag, and pulls out wanga. Fluffing up to do her show.*) And now, with a wave of my wanga . . . (MUNCHKINS *run to* S.L. *for safety.* DOROTHY *also follows to far* S.L.) I'm gonna disappear on you.(*Orchestra tone.*) I'm just gonna wave this thing three or four times . . . in ever increasing . . . (*The wanga turns into two handerchiefs.*) Now what the hell's goin' on around here? (*She picks up her bag, stuffing the two handerchiefs into it.*) Trouble is, honey, I ain't been disappearin' much lately. I been takin' the bus.

MUSIC #5A: *ADDAPERLE'S EXIT*

(*On the word "bus" a huge cloud of CO_2 vapor comes from* R-1, *and covers* ADDAPERLE'S *exit. The* MUNCHKINS *are all delighted and move toward* S.R., *with the* THIRD MUNCHKIN *furthest* D.R., *and the others in a semi-circle, above him: The* FOURTH, FIFTH, FIRST, *and* SECOND.)

THIRD MUNCHKIN. Addaperle's done done it again, y'all.
DOROTHY. (*Crossing* S.R. *and addressing the* FOURTH MUNCHKIN.) But she didn't tell me how to get to Emerald City.
FOURTH MUNCHKIN. (*Almost in tears.*) Oh, Darling!
FIRST MUNCHKIN. You can't miss it.
DOROTHY. (*Turning to her.*) I can't?
FIFTH MUNCHKIN. No.
SECOND MUNCHKIN. You see that road of yellow bricks?

(FOUR DANCERS *enter from* L-1, *dressed as the* YELLOW BRICK ROAD, *carrying staffs with which they will point the way to* DOROTHY. *She looks at them in bewilderment.*)

DOROTHY. Right . . .
SECOND MUNCHKIN. Just follow that for two days, now . . .
DOROTHY. (*Crossing to* YELLOW BRICK ROAD.) Right!
THIRD MUNCHKIN. But watch out for alot of spooky things!
DOROTHY. (*Stops, turning back to* MUNCHKINS.) Like what?
FOURTH MUNCHKIN. Beware of those awful Kalidah people!
(DOROTHY *crosses* D.S. *of the* ROAD *and to the* S.L. *side of it through the next three lines.*)
FIRST MUNCHKIN. Watch out for them terrible flying monkeys!
THIRD MUNCHKIN. (*Crosses in a bit.*) Most of all, watch out for that evil old Wicked Witch of the West! (*Looks around, just in case she's behind him.*) That girl is everything!
SECOND MUNCHKIN. (*As though no warnings had been given.*) Outside of that, have a nice trip!

MUSIC #6   *"SOON AS I GET HOME"*

(*With the musical intro, the tent pulls off* L-2, *and the* MUNCHKINS *pull the porch off also* L-2, *as the tent has cleared. The small section of the wall separates toward* S.L., *and out of the large section, a bridge opens, with a crow perched on it.* THE MUNCHKINS *have waved goodbye to* DOROTHY *through their exit,* DOROTHY *waves back, moves into the center of the* ROAD, *beginning her journey, just a bit apprehensive of it all.*)

DOROTHY.
THERE'S A FEELING HERE INSIDE
    (*All cross* S.R., ROAD *twirling staffs.*)
THAT I CANNOT HIDE
AND I KNOW I'VE TRIED
BUT IT'S TURNING ME AROUND

I'M NOT SURE THAT I'M AWARE
IF I'M UP OR DOWN
IF I'M HERE OR THERE
I NEED BOTH FEET ON THE GROUND
    (*They stop.*)

WHY DO I FEEL LIKE I'M DROWNING
    (DOROTHY *crosses* U.S.R.)
WHEN THERE IS PLENTY OF AIR?
WHY DO I FEEL LIKE FROWNING?
I THINK THE FEELING IS FEAR.

OH, HERE I AM IN A DIFFERENT PLACE
IN A DIFFERENT TIME
IN THIS TIME AND SPACE
BUT I DON'T WANT TO BE HERE
    (*On* "HERE," U.S. ROAD *puts pole down diagonally behind* DOROTHY.)
I WAS TOLD I MUST SEE THE WIZ
BUT I DON'T KNOW WHAT A WIZARD IS
    (*On* "IS," *second pole down.*)
I JUST HOPE THE WIZ IS THERE.

MAYBE I'M JUST GOING CRAZY
    (*On* "CRAZY," *third pole down.*)
LETTING MYSELF GET UP TIGHT
I'M ACTING JUST LIKE A BABY
    (*On* "BABY," *fourth pole down.*)
I'M GONNA BE ALRIGHT

SOON AS I GET HOME
SOON AS I GET HOME.
    (*Orchestra: Seque into* "HOME" [*Time signature change from 3/4 to 4/4*])
IN A DIFFERENT PLACE
IN A DIFFERENT TIME
DIFFERENT PEOPLE AROUND ME
    (DOROTHY *crosses* D.L., *and is stopped by* ROAD *with pole.*)
I WOULD LIKE TO KNOW OF THEIR
    (ROAD *points* D.R.C.)
DIFFERENT WORLD
AND HOW DIFFERENT THEY FIND ME
    (DOROTHY *crosses* D.R., ROAD *follows, forming diagonal* U.R. *to* D.C.)
AND JUST WHAT'S A WIZ, IS IT BIG?
    (DOROTHY *ducks under first pole.*)
WILL IT SCARE ME?
    (*Over second pole.*)
IF I ASK TO LEAVE, WILL THE WIZ
EVEN HEAR ME?
    (*Under third pole on* "THE WIZ.")
AND HOW WILL I KNOW THEN
    (*Under fourth pole* "AND.")
IF I'LL GET HOME AGAIN?
    (*Kneels* D.C.)

HERE I AM ALONE, THOUGH IT FEELS THE SAME
    (DOROTHY *up,* ROAD *forms behind her.*)
I DON'T KNOW WHERE I'M GOING
    (*On* "KNOW," *she falls back supported by two poles.*)
I'M HERE ON MY OWN, AND IT'S NOT A GAME
    (*On* "GAME," *she grasps the other two poles which have moved* D.S., *forming what in her mind is a trap.*)
AND A STRANGE WIND IS BLOWING
    (*On* "BLOWING," S.R. *pole spin* U.S.)
I AM SO AMAZED BY THE THINGS THAT I SEE HERE
    (*On* "AMAZED," *she circles around the* S.L. *pole . . . on* "THINGS," *she crosses* S.R. *to another pole.*)
I DON'T WANT TO BE AFRAID, I JUST DON'T WANT
TO BE HERE
IN MY MIND, THIS IS CLEAR
    (*Circling around that pole.*)

WHAT AM I DOING HERE?
> (*Sinking to the floor, using pole for support.*)

I WISH I WAS HOME.
> (*Collapses on deck, head toward* S.L. ROAD *spins out to dress stage.*)

ACT ONE

SCENE 2

A cornfield. The next instant.

THREE CROWS *enter from* R-1, *cawing loudly, and fluttering around* DOROTHY. *Frightened, she runs to* D.L., *shooing them away as she goes. They proceed to eat tidbits from each of the four* YELLOW BRICK ROAD *members, who are spaced* D.R., U.R. *against the large wall,* U.C. *against the small wall, and* D.L.

A SCARECROW *perched high on a pole rolls in from* R-3, *and stops* U.R.C., *just* U.S. *of the bridge joining the two walls.*

DOROTHY *has not seen him yet.*

SCARECROW. Psst!!

DOROTHY. (*Looking around, sees him, and rejects what she thinks she has heard.*) No, I know scarecrows can't talk.

SCARECROW. (*Calling to* DOROTHY.) Hey, honey! (DOROTHY *looks around, eye contact.*) You got any spare change?

DOROTHY. What?

SCARECROW. I said, you got any spare change? Some loose bread? Anything, till I get my head together?

DOROTHY. (*Crossing to* L. *of* C.) Now what would a scarecrow do with money?

SCARECROW. Well, I've been savin' up to buy me some brains.

DOROTHY. That's silly. You can't buy brains.

SCARECROW. (*A double-take.*) You can't??

DOROTHY. (*Sitting* L. *of* C.) No?

SCARECROW. Well, how about that?

DOROTHY. What do you want brains for? Isn't it any fun being a scarecrow?

SCARECROW. Well, I *thought* it would be. But after fifteen minutes up on this pole, I knew I wasn't going anyplace!

DOROTHY. (*Getting up.*) Scarecrow, how would you like to get *down* off that pole? (CROWS *carry on.*)

SCARECROW. (*Beaming.*) I thought you'd never ask! (*As* DOROTHY *crosses to the* S.L. *side of the* SCARECROW *unit under the bridge.*) Just pull on that vine down there. (DOROTHY *does so, and the* SCARECROW *is released, tumbling down onto the bridge, and then down to the stage floor. He is unable, for the moment, to maintain his balance, and is floppy, does three splits, spins around on his buns, falls face down, gets up, and finally strikes a pose* D.L.C. *He has been laughing all the time. As the* SCARECROW *has gone through the above, the* THREE CROWS *have cawed, and moved far* S.L., *finally settling* U.C.) Man, it sure feels good to stand on my own two feet again! (*He takes one step toward* DOROTHY, *and falls flat on his face.* DOROTHY *tries to pick him up, but he's all limp. She is* S.R. *of him.*)

DOROTHY. I guess you haven't had it easy, have you?

SCARECROW. Honey, you know it!

MUSIC #7: "I WAS BORN ON THE DAY BEFORE YESTERDAY"

SCARECROW. (*Up on his elbows. The* CROWS *still* U.S., *picking at* ROAD.)
(WOO WOO WOO
WOO WOO WOO)
(DOROTHY *spins him around to a sitting pose.*)
I WAS BORN ON THE DAY BEFORE YESTERDAY

I HAD HOLES IN MY SHOES, I WAS CRYING THE
    BLUES
    (*On "BLUES" left knee up.*)
AND I DIDN'T HAVE NO PLACE TO STAY
    (*On "NO PLACE" right knee up. On "STAY," CROWS pick him up.*)

BUT SOMEHOW I KNOW
I KNOW, I'M GONNA MAKE IT THIS TIME
YES, SOMEHOW I KNOW
I KNOW I'M GONNA MAKE IT THIS TIME, YEAH.

(*The* THREE CROWS *now move* D.S. *forming a singing and dancing chorus for him to work with.*)

I WAS BORN ON A HILL NOT SO FAR AWAY
OUT OF THREE RUBBER BANDS AND OLD GLOVES
    FOR HANDS,
AND A SUIT THAT HAD BEEN THROWN AWAY
THEY TOOK THE JACKET AND PANTS
FOUND A BROWN PAPER BAG
AND THEY FILLED IT WITH STRAW
AND TO TOP OFF THE DRAG
THEY GAVE ME PENCILLED-IN EYES
AND A PENCILLED-IN NOSE
AND THEY STUCK ME UP THERE AND SAID
STRIKE ME A POSE!!
    (*Pose.*)
BUT SOMEHOW I KNOW, I KNOW I'M
GONNA MAKE IT THIS TIME.
YES, SOMEHOW I KNOW (I KNOW)
I'M GONNA MAKE IT THIS TIME.
(THIS TIME I'M GONNA MAKE IT)
TELL ME
(WOO WOO WOO)
LET ME SING ONE
(WOO WOO WOO)
SO WE ALL CAN HEAR IT
(WOO WOO WOO)
GONNA LIFT MY HEAD UP
(WOO WOO WOO)
CAN YOU FEEL MY SPIRIT?
CAN YOU FEEL MY SPIRIT?

AND NOW THAT I KNOW
THAT I WASN'T BORN YESTERDAY
AND THAT I'M FULLY GROWN
I CAN STAND ON MY OWN
AND NOTHIN'S GONNA GET IN MY WAY

BECAUSE I'M GONNA GET MINE
GONNA TURN THINGS AROUND
GONNA GET MYSELF TOGETHER
GONNA GET ON DOWN
AND WHEN I FEEL THAT RAIN COME IN

THROUGH THE BOTTOM OF MY SHOES
I'M GONNA LEAVE 'EM BY THE ROADSIDE
AND QUIT CRYING THE BLUES

'CAUSE I KNOW (I KNOW)
I KNOW I'M GONNA MAKE IT THIS TIME
YES, SOMEHOW I KNOW (I KNOW)
I KNOW I'M GONNA MAKE IT THIS TIME.

(WOO WOO WOO)
GONNA SING ONE,
(WOO WOO WOO)
SO YOU ALL CAN HEAR IT
(WOO WOO WOO)
GONNA LIFT MY HEAD UP
(WOO WOO WOO)
CAN YOU FEEL MY SPIRIT?
CAN YOU FEEL MY SPIRIT?
(WOO WOO WOO)

(SCARECROW *does somersault toward* D.R.C., *ending up in a pose on button of number.* DOROTHY *is* D.C. *At applause crest, she starts to leave, crossing toward the* L-1 *exit.* SCARECROW *calling after her, and she reaches* D.L.C.)

Say, girl, what's your name?

DOROTHY. (*Turning back.*) Dorothy.

SCARECROW. Where you headed for?

DOROTHY. (*Pointing toward* S.L.) To Emerald City. (*Crossing* S.R. *toward him.*) There's this great big powerful Wiz, and they say he can do miracles. (*Crossing to* C.) So he's gonna get me back to Kansas. (SCARECROW *struggles to get up.* DOROTHY *crosses back to him, and tries to help him up. An idea hits her.*) Hey, you know what?

SCARECROW. (*Still half prone, propped up on his elbows.*) Of course not. I don't know anything.

DOROTHY. Maybe he could get you some brains.

SCARECROW. (*This gets him up.*) Brains? You mean that?

DOROTHY. Yeah!

SCARECROW. (*Running* U.S. *to tell* CROWS. CROWS *scatter, cawing.*) I'm gonna get my brains!!! I'm gonna get my brains!!! (SCARECROW *crosses back to* S.R. *side of* DOROTHY, *suddenly poised and suave.*) I hope my hat can handle it!!

ACT ONE

SCENE 3

On the YELLOW BRICK ROAD, *the next instant.*

MUSIC #8: *"EASE ON DOWN THE ROAD"*

YELLOW BRICK ROAD
COME ON, EASE ON DOWN, EASE ON DOWN THE
    ROAD
    (CROWS *exit* L-1.)
COME ON, EASE ON DOWN, EASE ON DOWN THE
    ROAD
DON'T YOU CARRY NOTHIN'
THAT MIGHT BE A LOAD
COME ON, EASE ON DOWN, EASE ON DOWN THE
    ROAD
    ALL.
COME ON, EASE ON DOWN, EASE ON DOWN THE
    ROAD
EASE ON DOWN, EASE ON DOWN THE ROAD
DON'T YOU CARRY NOTHIN'
THAT MIGHT BE A LOAD
COME ON, EASE ON DOWN, EASE ON DOWN THE
    ROAD

 CAUSE THERE MAY BE TIMES
WHEN YOU THINK YOU'VE LOST YOUR MIND
AND THE STEPS YOU'RE TAKING
LEAVE YOU THREE, FOUR STEPS BEHIND

JUST YOU KEEP ON KEEPIN'
ON THE ROAD THAT YOU CHOOSE, AND
DON'T YOU GIVE UP WALKING
'CAUSE YOU GAVE UP SHOES

EASE ON DOWN, EASE ON DOWN THE ROAD
COME ON, EASE ON DOWN, EASE ON DOWN THE
    ROAD
DON'T YOU CARRY NOTHIN'
THAT MIGHT BE A LOAD

COME ON
EASE ON DOWN, EASE ON DOWN
EASE ON DOWN, EASE ON DOWN
THE ROAD!!

(*The number ends with* DOROTHY *and* SCARECROW D.L. *The* YEL-LOW BRICK ROAD *points* D.L., *indicating that the way continues in that direction. From the vicinity of* U.R., *which is* U.S. *of the large wall, behind which a tree has flown in, we hear a groan.*)

DOROTHY. What was that? (*Another groan.* YELLOW BRICK ROAD *looks* U.R. *also.*)

SCARECROW. It's coming from over there! (*Points* U.R.)

DOROTHY. What should we do?

SCARECROW. (*Pointing* D.L., *and crossing* D.S. *of her.*) Go over there!!

DOROTHY. (*Turning him around to face the sound, she is now* D.S. *of him.*) No. Scarecrow, somebody needs help. (DOROTHY *and* SCARECROW *move* U.S. *as the large wall moves toward* S.L., *revealing the* TINMAN *standing at the base of a large tree far* U.R. *He is rusted solid.* SCARECROW *gets* U.S. *of* TINMAN, *and rocking him back and forth, from one leg to the other, walks him* D.S. *to* D.R.C. *With each move, we hear a rusty squeak from the orchestra. They examine him,* SCARECROW *on the right of* TINMAN, DOROTHY *on the left. The* YELLOW BRICK ROAD *faces* U.S.)

DOROTHY. What is it?

SCARECROW. Don't look an "is" to me. Looks more like a "was."

TINMAN. (*A rusted cry.*) Oil! (SCARECROW *and* DOROTHY *jump back in fright.*) Oil! (SCARECROW *and* DOROTHY *move in to hear.*) I need oil . . . oil . . . oil . . .

DOROTHY. (*Talking through* TINMAN *to* SCARECROW.) He needs oil!

TINMAN. (*Turning to* DOROTHY, *much effort and squeaks, very mechanical, three big moves.* DOROTHY *leans back.*) Oh, please, miss . . . there is some in that little shack . . . (*He moves to tilt* D.S. *to see shack,* DOROTHY *tilts* U.S. *in counter.* TINMAN *indicates* L-1 *exit.*)

DOROTHY. I'll get it! (*She runs off* L-1.)

SCARECROW. (*He follows to* L.C.) No, Dorothy, wait! (*He looks back to* S.R., *then to* S.L., *then back to* S.R. *His arms swing loosely in the breeze. Finally mustering his courage, the* SCARECROW *moves*

toward the TINMAN, *falling flat on his face, just* D.S. *of* TINMAN.
SCARECROW *moves on all fours to* S.R. *of* TINMAN, *getting up slowly,
giving him the once-over as he rises.* TINMAN, *with great effort,
squeaks and turns to greet* SCARECROW, *now on his right.*)

TINMAN. (*When their eyes meet.*) Hi!

TINMAN. (*Jumps back in fright.*) Oh! (*Recovering.*) Man, I have
seen me some spaced-out garbage cans in my day . . . (DOROTHY
enters L-1 *with the oil can,* SCARECROW *turns away* S.R., *as*
DOROTHY *crosses to* TINMAN.)

DOROTHY. (*As she gets to* TINMAN, *she squirts oil into his mouth.*)
I found it, tinman. Now what?

TINMAN. Now what? (*The* YELLOW BRICK ROAD *relaxes and
faces the action in a casual group* U.L.)

MUSIC #9 *"SLIDE SOME OIL TO ME"*

(*During the song,* DOROTHY *follows his instructions as to where to
oil him. As she does so, he becomes looser and looser.*)

SLIDE SOME OIL TO ME
LET IT SLIP DOWN MY SPINE
    (DOROTHY *does spine.*)
IF YOU DON'T HAVE STP
CRISCO BE JUST FINE
    (DOROTHY *crosses* D.S. *to* S.R. *side,* SCARECROW *crosses* U.S. *to*
    S.L. *side, but remaining slightly* U.S.)

SLIDE SOME OIL TO ME
HIT MY SHOULDER BLADE
    (TINMAN *falls back,* SCARECROW *catches him and sets him back
    up straight; as* DOROTHY *oils his shoulder blade.*)
ALL Y'ALL THAT DON'T HAVE TO LUBRICATE
SURE HAVE GOT IT MADE.

SLIDE SOME OIL TO ME
SLIP SOME TO MY SIDE
    (DOROTHY *does.*)
STANDING HERE IN ONE POSITION
SURE CAN MAKE ONE TIRED

SLIP SOME TO MY ELBOWS
AND MY FINGERS, IF YOU WOULD

(TINMAN *gives his axe to* SCARECROW, *for whom it is too heavy.
He staggers under the weight toward* U.L., *giving the axe to the
Up Stage-most* YELLOW BRICK ROAD, *and then returns to the*
S.L. *side of* TINMAN.)
COME ON, SLIDE SOME OIL TO ME, GIRL
OOOH, DOES THAT FEEL GOOD

SLIDE SOME OIL TO MY FEET
        (DOROTHY *does.*)
LOOK, I HAVE TOES AGAIN
        (*Toes move.*)
COME ON AND SLIDE SOME OIL TO MY KNEES
        (DOROTHY *does.*)
AND LET ME SEE IF I CAN BEND
        (*Knees bend.*)
SLIDE SOME OIL TO ME
I'M BEGINNING TO FEEL FINE
COME ON AND SLIDE SOME OIL TO MY THROAT
        (DOROTHY *does.*)
AND LET ME LUBRICATE MY MIND
AND LET ME LUBRICATE MY MIND
AND LET ME LUBRICATE MY MIND
        (*Dance Section.* TINMAN *lose balance.*)
Help!
        (TINMAN *crosses to* SCARECROW, *starts to fall,* SCARECROW
        catches him and sets him upright again.)
SLIDE SOME OIL TO ME
I'M BEGINNING TO FEEL FINE
        (DOROTHY *takes the oilcan to the base of the scenic wall* U.L.)
COME ON AND SLIDE SOME OIL TO MY THROAT
        (DOROTHY *takes oil can to base of large wall.*)
AND LET ME LUBRICATE MY MIND
        (TINMAN *crosses* L., SCARECROW *follows.*)
AND LET ME LUBRICATE MY MIND
AND LET ME
        (*Dance.*)
LUBRICATE MY MIND.
        (*Dance.*)
    DOROTHY. Hit it, Tin Man.
        (*Dance.*)
    DOROTHY. Wait for me.
        (*During dance.*)

TINMAN. Come on, honey!
AND LET ME LUBRICATE MY MIND
AND LET ME LUBRICATE
LET ME LUBRICATE MY MIND
MY MIND!

(*The number ends with the three of them* D.L.C. DOROTHY *is to the* R.
of the TINMAN, SCARECROW *to the* L. TINMAN, *in gratitude,
kisses* DOROTHY'S *hand.*)

SCARECROW. (*Reaches across* TINMAN *and grabs* DOROTHY'S
hand, pulls her toward the L-1 *exit.*) Come on, Dorothy, we gotta be
going.
DOROTHY. (*Pulls her hand free, and returns to* TINMAN.) Wait
a minute. How did you ever get that way?
TINMAN. Well, I wasn't always made outta tin, you know.
DOROTHY. No?
TINMAN. No! I used to be a real flesh and blood woodchopper, 'til
one day a wicked old witch put a spell on my axe.

(*During the preceding line, the* SCARECROW *has become interested
and crossed in to* L. *of* DOROTHY. *At the news of a "spell on his
axe," the* YELLOW BRICK ROAD *panics, and trembling, passes
the axe* D.S. *from one* MEMBER *to the next, then turns* U.S.)

DOROTHY. A spell!
TINMAN. (*Seeing the* YELLOW BRICK ROAD *coming unglued
crosses to the* D.S.-*most member and* . . .) Yeah! And she really
did some number . . . [*Gets the axe.*] Let me tell you. (*Returns to*
S.L. *side of* DOROTHY *to continue story.*) I mean, one day when I was
choppin' down a tree . . . (*The* YELLOW BRICK ROAD *turns back
in to listen.*) that axe slipped (*Slaps thigh with axe, straightens leg.*)
and cut off my left leg.
SCARECROW. (*Holding onto* DOROTHY *in fear.*) MMMM!! Ain't
that somethin'?
TINMAN. (*Quick pick-up.*) Yeah. I thought so. So I went to this
here Tinsmith I knew, and I said: "Hey, man . . . do you think
you could fix me up with a tin leg? (*Addressing tinsmith as though he
were* D.C., *in audience.*) Well, he did. (*Laugh.*) And the next day
I'm back choppin', doin' my thing, and damn, if that old axe don't
slip . . . (*Slaps right thigh with axe, straightens leg.*) and cut off
my right leg! So I go back to the tinsmith and get me another leg.

SCARECROW. (*Crossing on line below* TINMAN *and to his left.*) Now at no time did it dawn on you to get yourself a new axe?

TINMAN. (*Lifts the axe in a threat to the* SCARECROW. DOROTHY *restrains him,* TINMAN *relaxes, smiles to* SCARECROW *that the threat was unintentional.*) Well, before I knew what was happening, bit by bit . . .(TINMAN *taps his head twice, then his chest twice.*) I was all tin. And that's the way it all come about.

DOROTHY. (*Crosses in, touches him.*) You poor man.

TINMAN. Well, you can't have everything.

SCARECROW. (*Step in toward* TINMAN.) An' that's the truth!

(*As* TINMAN *turns toward* SCARECROW, DOROTHY *crosses* U.S. *to get the oil can, and then returns to the* S.R. *side of the* TINMAN.)

TINMAN. (*Raising his right hand in a vow.*) God's honest truth!

SCARECROW. Cross your heart!

TINMAN. (*Starts to cross heart with right hand, then stops.*) No . . . I can't do that.

SCARECROW. (*Crossing* D.S. *of* TINMAN, *grabs* DOROTHY's *right hand, pulling her across to* D.R.C.) I knew it. You was jivin' us all along. C'mon, Dorothy.

TINMAN. (*Following them, with great urgency.*) No, no! Wait, wait! (DOROTHY *and* SCARECROW *stop.*) I can't cross my heart, (TINMAN *crosses* L. *to* L. *of* C.) 'cause I don't have no heart.

DOROTHY. (*Crosses down to his* R.) You don't have a heart?

TINMAN. (*Turning to* DOROTHY.) Well, it didn't come with the suit. (SCARECROW *crosses in.*) You know, nowadays . . . (TINMAN *crosses* D.S. *and to his* L.) it isn't enough just being (*Pose, lean on axe.*) good looking.

DOROTHY. (*Holds a momentary conference with* SCARECROW, *then:*) Then come with us to the Emerald City . . . (*On the words "Emerald City,"* the YELLOW BRICK ROAD *reforms facing* U.S., *on a diagonal* S.L.) . . . and see the Wiz. They say he can do most anything for anybody.

TINMAN. Yeah? (*Spins counter-clockwise, and laughs.*) Just show me the way.

MUSIC #10: "*EASE ON DOWN THE ROAD*" (Reprise)

DOROTHY, SCARECROW, YELLOW BRICK ROAD.
PICK YOUR RIGHT FOOT UP
WHEN YOUR LEFT ONE'S DOWN

COME ON, LEGS KEEP MOVIN'
DON'T YOU LOSE NO GROUND
'CAUSE THE ROAD YOU'RE WALKIN'
MIGHT BE LONG SOMETIME
BUT JUST KEEP ON STEPPIN'
AND YOU'LL BE JUST FINE . . .
    DOROTHY, SCARECROW, TINMAN.
COME ON AND EASE ON DOWN THE ROAD
COME ON, EASE ON DOWN, EASE ON DOWN
    THE ROAD
DON'T YOU CARRY NOTHIN'
THAT MIGHT BE A LOAD
COME ON
EASE ON DOWN, EASE ON DOWN THE ROAD
    LION. (*Mighty roar.*)

ACT ONE

SCENE 4

Down the road a piece. The next instant.

An O.S. *roar interrupts the journey of* DOROTHY, SCARECROW, TINMAN, *and the* YELLOW BRICK ROAD.

The THREE FRIENDS *scatter to* D.R., *the* YELLOW BRICK ROAD *freezes* U.R.C., *hiding behind their staffs.*

MUSIC #11:   Seque to "*MEAN OLE LION*"

(*To a beat, the* COWARDLY LION *appears, strutting his false courage, and trying to intimidate everyone. He enters from* L-1.)

    LION. (*Two mighty roars take him to* D.C.)
SAY WHAT YOU WANNA
BUT I'M HERE TO STAY
I'M A MEAN OLE LION.
    (*Crosses* L.C.)
YOU CAN GO WHERE YOU WANNA
BUT DON'T GET IN MY WAY
I'M A MEAN OLE LION.
    (*Crosses* R. *to* C.)

YOU'LL BE STANDING IN A DRAFT
IF YOU DON'T HEAR ME LAUGH
AND IF YOU HAVE TO COME AROUND
BETTER HOPE THAT I DON'T FROWN
'CAUSE I JUST MIGHT KNOCK YOU DOWN
CUZ I'M A MEAN OLE LION.
(*Crosses* s.l., *roars at* YELLOW BRICK ROAD, *who scatters toward* s.r., *forming a diagonal from* u.c. *to* d.r.c. TINMAN *takes cover behind the* u.s.-*most* YELLOW BRICK ROAD, *the next* YELLOW BRICK ROAD d.s. *has no one hiding behind him, the third* YELLOW BRICK ROAD *hides the* SCARECROW, *and the* D.S.-*most* YELLOW BRICK ROAD *shelters* DOROTHY. *All their knees knock in terror, except for the* TINMAN. *The* LION *is now* U.L., *and crosses* D.C.)
DON'T YOU KNOW I'M READY TO FIGHT
I'LL TURN YOUR DAY INTO NIGHT
I'M A MEAN OLE LION
(*Backs to* D.L.)
AND IF YOU'RE HALF BRIGHT
YOU'LL DETOUR TO THE RIGHT
I'M A MEAN OLE LION
(*Crosses* R.)

ALL YOU STRANGERS BETTER BEWARE
THIS IS THE KING OF THE JUNGLE HERE
(*Underplayed, and spoken.*)
AND IF I HAPPEN TO LET YOU SLIDE
DON'T JUST STAND THERE, RUN AND HIDE
(*Said threateningly to* YELLOW BRICK ROAD *and* FRIENDS *who run to* D.R. *in a cluster for mutual protection.*)
NOW, YOU JUST CAUGHT MY BETTER SIDE
I'M A MEAN OLE LION
MEAN OLE LION!

(*At the end of the number, the* LION *ends up* D.C., *and is very aware of the applause, and reacts to it like a ham actor, milking it for all he's worth. He swings his tail, then as the applause starts to die, he beckons for more. In the meantime, the* SCARECROW *and the* TINMAN *re-assess their attitude toward the* LION, *and decide that the initial reaction wasn't called for.*)

SCARECROW. (*Crossing in a bit.*) Well, he don't scare me. (*The*

YELLOW BRICK ROAD *crosses* U.R., *facing* D.S. *and are* D.S. *of the tree.* SCARECROW *asks* TINMAN.) Do he scare you?

TINMAN. (*Crossing in to about two feet from* SCARECROW.) No way, man, no way.

(*The* LION, *noticing their disrespectful attitude, runs over and throws* SCARECROW *to* D.L.C., *on his belly, and swats the* TINMAN *in the side, knocking him to the* S.R. *portal leg, and hurting his hand.* DOROTHY, *in an attempt to protect her friends, takes a roundhouse punch at the* LION, *actually hitting him in the chest, and decks him. As he lands and falls flat, and starts sitting up,* DOROTHY *advances on him, but not past his feet.*)

LION. (*At* C.S. *where he has landed.*) Don't hit me no more!!

TINMAN. (*A step in toward* C.) Will you dig that?

LION. (*On all fours, crawls* U.S. *and slightly* S.L.) Don't you know you could hurt a person (*To* SCARECROW.) that way?

SCARECROW. (*Breaking up, and rolling* S.L.) And you call yourself the king of the jungle? (TINMAN *also laughs.*)

LION. (*Rises, advancing on* SCARECROW *whose laugh dies with* LION's *approach.*) You don't see no other cat begging for the gig, do you? (LION *growls,* SCARECROW *jumps in fear, scaring* LION.)

TINMAN. (*Crossing to* R. *of* LION.) Man, you've got a yellow streak a mile wide!

LION. (*Highly indignant, and very grand.*) It is not!! It's my mane. I just had it touched up this morning. (*On "touched,"* LION *crosses to* R. *of* C., *moving* D.S. *of* DOROTHY *as he passes her.*)

DOROTHY. (*At* S.L. *of* LION.) You coward!! Goin' around roarin' at people. (LION *pulls away* S.R. *a bit.*) You ought to be ashamed . . . (DOROTHY *spanks* LION.)

LION. (*Growl* . . . DOROTHY *doesn't budge.*) I am. DOROTHY *turns* S.L.) But it's not my fault. (DOROTHY *moves away* L. *to* TINMAN, *and both of them and* SCARECROW *turn away* S.L. *having nothing to do with the* LION.) No, wait!! (LION *moves* S.L., D.S. *of the group finally ending up* D.L.C.) I was an only cub. Daddy left home when I was born, and Momma was such a strong lady. It was either "do this" or "don't do that" . . . "you call them paws clean?" . . . (DOROTHY, TINMAN, *and* SCARECROW *now interested, move in to the* S.R. *side of the* LION. *The* SCARECROW *stays a bit* U.S. *of* LION.) "Lick behind your ears, child, or you don't get no dessert." And all I ever got was a bunch of schizophobic phrenias . . .

SCARECROW. (*Crossing* U.S. *of* LION *and to his* L.) Wow!! (LION *jumps.*) Where'd you get all them big words from?

LION. My owl.

TINMAN. (S.R. *of* LION.) What owl??

LION. (*Pulling a mimed pill box out of his left trouser pocket.*) I've been seeing a high-priced owl for three years now.

DOROTHY. An owl?

LION. Yes, an owl. (*Popping pills like mad.*) An hour each time. You don't realize what kind of bread that runs into.

SCARECROW. And this here . . . uh . . . owl. What's he say in the answer to your disgraceful self?

LION. Owls don't give answers. They just ask questions. Like Whoo? Whoo? (SCARECROW *crosses* U.S. *of group to the* S.R. *side of* TINMAN, *perplexed.*) So at heart . . . (LION *crosses* D.S. *a bit.*) . . . I'll never be anything but a big ole scaredy-cat. (LION *starts to cry.*)

TINMAN. (*Very sympathetic, crosses in to* LION . . .) Awww! (. . . TINMAN *puts his left arm over* LION's *shoulder* . . . LION *screams and jumps* S.L.) It could be worse. At least you got a heart. (DOROTHY *turns out in thought.*)

SCARECROW. And at least you got a brain. Even if it is making him a pretty mixed-up cat.

LION. (*Crossing* S.L. *a bit, lots of self-pity.*) What good's a heart? What good's a brain? If you ain't got no courage?

DOROTHY. (*She crosses in to* LION, D.S. *of* TINMAN *and* SCARECROW.) You know, maybe . . . (DOROTHY *takes* LION *a bit further* D.L., *so he won't be embarrassed by the others.*) . . . just maybe, if you came with us and saw the great Wiz, he could give you some courage . . . just like that. (*Snaps fingers.*)

LION. (*Like an aside.*) In only one session? (DOROTHY *nods* "yes," TINMAN *and* SCARECROW *do one shake of hands* . . . LION *crosses* S.R., *until he is* S.R. *of* TINMAN *and* SCARECROW, *turns back to them.*) Gentlemen . . . (*Crosses left to between* DOROTHY *and* TINMAN.) Little Momma, of course . . . (*To all.*) may I fill out your foursome?

MUSIC #12: *"EASE ON DOWN THE ROAD"* (Reprise)

DOROTHY, TINMAN, SCARECROW.
COME ON
EASE ON DOWN, EASE ON DOWN THE ROAD
COME ON
EASE ON DOWN, EASE ON DOWN THE ROAD

DON'T YOU CARRY NOTHIN'
THAT MIGHT BE A LOAD
COME ON
EASE ON DOWN, EASE ON DOWN THE ROAD
  YELLOW BRICK ROAD.
YOU'LL BE SORRY!!
  DOROTHY, SCARECROW, TINMAN.
CUZ THERE MAY BE TIMES
WHEN YOU WISH YOU WASN'T BORN
AND YOU WAKE ONE MORNING
JUST TO FIND YOUR COURAGE GONE

BUT JUST KNOW THAT FEELIN'
ONLY LASTS A LITTLE WHILE
AND JUST STICK WITH US
AND WE'LL SHOW YOU HOW TO SMILE . . .

COME ON . . .
    (LION *joins others in lyric*)

EASE ON DOWN, EASE ON DOWN THE ROAD
COME ON
EASE ON DOWN, EASE ON DOWN THE ROAD
DON'T YOU CARRY NOTHIN'
    (*The* YELLOW BRICK ROAD *starts to break toward* S.R., *but the* FOUR
    FRIENDS *are so engrossed in "Easing on Down," they don't
    notice.*)

THAT MIGHT BE A LOAD
COME ON
EASE ON DOWN, EASE ON DOWN . . .
EASE ON DOWN, EASE ON DOWN . . .
EASE ON DOWN, EASE ON DOWN

    (*Ad lib continues, as it gets darker. The* YELLOW BRICK ROAD
    has exited S.R. *during the repeated "EASE ON DOWN," and
    the* FOUR FRIENDS *are now alone.*)

ACT ONE

SCENE 5

A funky part of the forest, a little later.

The LION *is* R. *of* C., DOROTHY *is at* C., SCARECROW S.L. *of*
DOROTHY, TINMAN, S.L. *of him.*

LION. (*Yelling out, to get their attention.*) Wait a minute, y'all.
Where are we? (LION *moves in toward group.* DOROTHY *and*
SCARECROW *hold on to each other.*)
SCARECROW. I think we're lost.
LION. (*Crossing in.*) What makes you say that?
SCARECROW. (*Crossing* D.S. DOROTHY *to* LION.) 'Cause you don't
know where we are.
DOROTHY. (*Looking around for possible directions, heads* D.S. *a
bit, slightly to* S.R., *and points* D.S.) Then let's go . . . this way.

(*The others fall in next to her, the* LION S.R., DOROTHY R.C.,
SCARECROW L.C, TINMAN S.L. *They mime a walk in place. We
hear the sounds of birds, insects, and other spooky things.*)

DOROTHY, LION, SCARECROW, TINMAN. (*Very feebly, and
terrified.*)
EASE ON DOWN, EASE ON DOWN THE ROAD
EASE ON DOWN, EASE ON DOWN THE ROAD . . .

(DOROTHY *looks to her* S.R., *and sees the first two* STRANGERS *who
have entered* R-1, *about to cross* D.S. *of the* FOUR FRIENDS.)

DOROTHY. Look!! (LION *pulls her back. The first two* STRANGERS,
dressed in huge hoop skirts, cross D.S., *never taking their eyes off
where they are going. They carry windchime type rattles.*)
TINMAN. (*About the second* STRANGER, *a lady.*) This one's got
rhythm. (*The second pair of* STRANGERS *have entered, also from*
R-1, *holding heart-shaped masks in front of their faces. They also
pay no attention to the* FOUR FRIENDS, *passing* D.S. *of them, and
follow the* FIRST COUPLE *off* L-1.)
SCARECROW. (*About the third* STRANGER, *also a lady.*) There's a
little ugly one. (*The last* STRANGER *enters from* L-1, *a man in a huge
white gown, white hat, carrying two dumb-bell type batons, and
laughing maniacally, passes as did the two* COUPLES *before him.*)
LION. Oh, Momma!!
TINMAN. (*As last* STRANGER *passes him.*) It can't be Halloween.
(*Another laugh from the last* STRANGER *just before he exits* L-1.)
LION. I'm sorry, Momma. I didn't mean it.
DOROTHY. (*Crosses* D.S.) Why is it getting so dark?
SCARECROW. Beats me.

TINMAN. (*Crosses* L.C.) It's nowhere near sundown yet.

LION. I know!! (*They all run to him.*) This is the part of the forest where those Kalidahs live.

DOROTHY. What's a Kalidah?

LION. I was afraid you was gonna ask me that.

MUSIC #13: *"KALIDAH BATTLE"*

(*The* FOUR FRIENDS *runs* U.R., *around the tree, when they spy the* KALIDAH QUEEN *riding on the shoulders of two of her* GANG, *and being pulled by four* OTHERS. *The* KALIDAHS *have long noses, grotesque long fingernails and are intent on destroying* DOROTHY *and her* FRIENDS. *The* FOUR FRIENDS *run to* D.L., *when the* KALIDAHS *overtake them.* ONE *picks up* DOROTHY, *and tries to run off* S.R. *with her, however she is saved by the* SCARECROW. *The* KALIDAH QUEEN *leaps upon the* LION, *who falls with her* L.C., *and they rock back and forth in combat, until either the* TINMAN, *or the* SCARECROW *beats all of them off, and they exit* S.R. *and* S.L. *The battle ends with the* SCARECROW U.R., DOROTHY D.R.C., LION L.C., *and the* TINMAN S.L.)

ACT ONE

SCENE 6

A poppy field, a few minutes later.

TINMAN. (*Crossing in* U.S. *of* LION *who is still down.*) Come on, man.

LION. (*Screams, crosses on all fours toward* DOROTHY R.C.) Oh, Momma, that you, Momma?

DOROTHY. (*To comfort.*) Lion. (SCARECROW *crosses in from* U.R., *toward* TINMAN. *They meet* U.S. *and* L. *of* DOROTHY *and* LION.)

LION. That was too close for comfort.

DOROTHY. (*Kneeling* S.L. *of* LION.) Tinman.

TINMAN. (*Crosses in to* DOROTHY.) Yes, Honey.

DOROTHY. You sure saved us all.

TINMAN. Aw, it wasn't no big thing.

DOROTHY. And, Scarecrow, you sure kept your cool, too.

SCARECROW. (*Crosses in to* DOROTHY, D.S. *of* TINMAN.) What can I say? (*Does hand slap with* DOROTHY. DOROTHY *now looks at*

LION, *who expects some congratulations also. But* DOROTHY *merely looks to the others* S.L.)

LION. (*Highly insulted, turns to* S.R., *the martyr.*) That's right. The offense always gets the headlines. Nobody ever talks about the defense any more.

SCARECROW. And what kind of defense were you doin', O Mighty King of the Jungle?

LION. The king of defense only kings can do.

TINMAN. (*Crossing in to between* DOROTHY *and* SCARECROW.) And what's that?

LION. (*Very grand.*) King Fu!!

SCARECROW *and* TINMAN. (*Collapsing hysterically in each others' arms.*) King Fu????

DOROTHY. (*Up from comforting* LION, *advances on* TINMAN *and* SCARECROW.) No, wait a minute. I know my lion was more scared than anybody, but he saved me three or four times. (*She goes back to the* S.L. *side of the* LION, *who now gets to his knees.*)

LION. Yeah! There you go, Jack, I sure did. And I would have done more in there, too, but right in the middle of it there, I got this furball!

DOROTHY. (*Busy fluffing him up.*) Yeah, he got a furball.

SCARECROW. (*Crossing* L. *to* L.C.) A furball?? Man, you are something else?

TINMAN. (*Crossing* U.S. *of* DOROTHY *and* LION, *and swats* LION *on fanny with side of axe on word "Pussy."*) You ain't nothing but a big ole pussycat. (TINMAN *backs* U.L., *dragging axe to torment* LION, *who goes after* TINMAN *as he moves away.*)

MUSIC #14:   *"BE A LION"*

TINMAN. (*Still in the cross* U.L.) Meow! Meow!

LION. (*Has crossed* D.S. *of* DOROTHY *and goes after* TINMAN, *but is no match.*) What do you know. You don't know anything about it . . . (LION *now returns to* C..) Yes. You're right. A big ole pussycat. I guess that's all I am. That's all I'll ever be. (*He is on the verge of tears.*)

DOROTHY. (*Kneels.*) No, you won't.

LION. (*Hopefully.*) I won't?

DOROTHY.
THERE IS A PLACE WE'LL GO
WHERE THERE IS MOSTLY QUIET
    (TINMAN *leans on his axe.*)

FLOWERS AND BUTTERFLIES
    (LION *crosses to* DOROTHY R.C.)
A RAINBOW LIVES BESIDE IT
    (SCARECROW *sits,* TINMAN *kneels* S.L., *which is behind him, puts arm over* SCARECROW'S *shoulders, a nice moment of comradeship.*)

AND FROM A VELVET SKY
    (LION *tries to put his head in* DOROTHY'S *lap.*)
A SUMMER STORM
I CAN FEEL THE COOLNESS IN THE AIR
BUT I'M STILL WARM

AND THEN A MIGHTY ROAR
WILL START THE SKY TO CRYING
NOT EVEN LIGHTNING
WILL BE FRIGHTENING MY LION
    (*Touch on "frightening."*)

AND WITH NO FEAR INSIDE
NO NEED TO RUN, NO NEED TO HIDE
YOU'RE STANDING STRONG AND TALL
    (DOROTHY *up on "standing."*)
YOU'RE THE BRAVEST OF THEM ALL
IF ON COURAGE YOU MUST CALL
THEN KEEP ON TRYIN' AND TRYIN' AND TRYIN'
YOU'RE A LION
IN YOU OWN WAY, BE A LION!

Come on, be a Lion!! (for me!)
    (DOROTHY *helps* LION *to stand.*)

    DOROTHY & LION.
I'M (YOU'RE) STANDING STRONG AND TALL
I'M (YOU'RE) THE BRAVEST OF THEM ALL
IF ON COURAGE YOU (I) MUST CALL
THEN I'LL (YOU'LL) KEEPING ON TRYIN'
AND TRYIN', AND TRYIN'
YOU'RE A LION
IN YOUR (MY) OWN WAY
I'M (BE) A LION!
    TINMAN. (*He looks* D.C., *and out over the audience, then he gets*

up excitedly and pointing.) Hey, look. Isn't that the Emerald City out there?

DOROTHY. (*Crosses* D.S. *to* R. *of* TINMAN, *looking* D.S.) Look how beautiful it is. (LION *crosses* U.S. *of group to* S.L. *end;* SCARECROW *crosses* U.S. *of group to* S.R. *end.*)

TINMAN. Incredible.

SCARECROW. (*Now* S.R. *of* DOROTHY.) Look at all that glitter! (*Five* POPPIES *enter from* S.L., *from the* D.S.-*most, to the* U.S.-*most entrances.*)

LION. I wonder if I can get a touch-up before we see the Wiz? (DOROTHY *crosses* U.S. *of* LION *to* S.L. *The* POPPIES *mingle among the* FOUR FRIENDS.)

TINMAN. Hey! What's all this?

SCARECROW. Just looks like a bunch of flowers to me.

MUSIC #15: "*LION'S DREAM*"

LION. (*Fascinated by the Girls.*) Yeah, and I suddenly have the urge to do a little cross-pollinating. (*Crosses* U.S. *Suddenly* DOROTHY *remembers* ADDAPERLE's *warning about the poppy field.*)

DOROTHY. (*From* D.L.) No! This is the poppy field. We gotta get out of here. (DOROTHY *crosses* S.R., *grabbing* SCARECROW *on the way, and heads for the* R-2 *exit, eventually leaving that way with* SCARECROW *and* TINMAN *in tow.*)

SCARECROW. Hold your nose!

TINMAN. Don't sniff that stuff.

LION. Wait for me! (*He starts to follow to* R-2, *but a* POPPY *blows dust in his face, and he is hooked.*) Y'all go on ahead. (*Crosses* D.L.C.) I'll bring up the rear! (*The* POPPIES, *beautiful, sinuous, like streetwalkers, radiating sex, surround the* LION. *He moves among them, trying to touch and sniff each one. He gets higher and higher.*) All together, ladies . . .

(*The* POPPIES *surround him, and grind and bump. Finally closing in, and do barrel rolls around him. As the second Girl gets up from her barrel roll, we hear a siren . . . and a paddy wagon, manned by four* FIELD MICE *enters from* L-3. *The* FIRST MOUSE *is perched on the seat like a coachman, with the* SECOND MOUSE *behind steering, and another on either side. The paddy wagon moves to* D.R.C., *where the* FIRST MOUSE *dismounts, and runs across to the* LION D.L.C. *At the sound of the siren, the* POPPIES *make a quick exit* L-1, *having been busted before.*

The MICE *chase them away, with the* FIRST MOUSE *the most aggressive. After the* POPPIES *are gone, the* MICE *surround the* LION, *who is still lying down, and flying high on poppy dust. The* FIRST MOUSE *returns to the* S.R. *side of the* LION, *the* SECOND MOUSE *on the* S.L. *side, the other two further* U.S. *backing up the* FIRST TWO.)

FIRST MOUSE. (*Said to the* POPPIES *as they are exiting.*) Okay, break it up. (*To the* S.R. *side of the* LION.) We're with the Mice Squad. I said, we're with the Mice Squad. (*Prods* LION *with his foot.*) Get up from there.

LION. (*Really high.*) The Mice Squad?

FIRST MOUSE. Yeah, the Mice Squad.

LION. (*Slowly rising, giggling to himself. The* THIRD MOUSE *opens the paddy wagon.*) Now, looka here . . . Mousifer . . . (LION *giggles some more.*) How come I can't never find me no mouse when I need one, baby?

FIRST MOUSE. Okay, buddy, now where'd you get those poppies from . . . (*Hops away, then back again.*) . . . huh???? (SECOND MOUSE *hops in closer.*)

LION. Poppies, poppies . . . Actually, I'm from out of town, sir. I came here with the Lions Club. . . .

SECOND MOUSE. Yeah! That's what they all say. (*He grabs* LION's *left arm, making the arrest.*)

FIRST MOUSE. (*Crossing* S.R. *to in front of the paddy wagon, but still directing operations.*) You're under arrest! Get in there! (*The* MICE *gets him into the wagon slamming the gate shut through:*)

LION. I didn't do nothin'. Hey, wait a minute. You ain't payin' for my clothes. I demand to see my owl. I said, I demand to see . . . (*They wheel him toward* S.L., *swing around heading to the* R-2 *exit, and we hear him cry, as the lights fade out* . . .) Momma, Momma, Momma . . .

MUSIC #15A: "BE A LION" TAG

ACT ONE

SCENE 7

Outside the gates of Emerald City. A little while later.

TINMAN, DOROTHY, *and* SCARECROW *enter, in that order, from*

D.L., *and to the opening in the* C. *of the scrim.* TINMAN *to the* S.R. *side of the gate,* DOROTHY S.L. *side, and* SCARECROW S.L. *of* DOROTHY.

TINMAN. (*Crossing to the gate.*) Dorothy! We're here! I don't believe Emerald City.

SCARECROW. Man, we finally made it through!

DOROTHY. Now all we got to do is find the Wiz.

TINMAN. (*Crossing* S.L. *to* L. *of* SCARECROW.) And the Lion. (*The* LION *enters* R-1, *sullenly, being prodded by the* FIRST MOUSE.)

FIRST MOUSE. C'mon, move it along there, buddy. (LION *crosses to* C. *and then* U.S. *to between* SCARECROW *and* DOROTHY.)

DOROTHY. There you are.

LION. (*Very grand.*) Wait 'til my owl hears about this.

TINMAN. What happened?

LION. I don't believe it. Me, the Kitty of the Kingdom, being busted by a mouse!

FIRST MOUSE. (*Really wants to chew somebody, crosses to* TINMAN, *who is on the* S.L. *side of the group.*) Look, I wanna tell ya, your cat there was really flying.

TINMAN. We're sorry, officer. Very sorry.

FIRST MOUSE. Well, just make sure he never goes in that poppy field again. Y'hear?

TINMAN. We'll do our best, sir. Thank you. (SCARECROW *looks at* MOUSE, *then crosses to the* S.R. *side of* DOROTHY. FIRST MOUSE *turns and exits* R-1, *hopping and squeaking all the way.* TINMAN *crosses* U.S. *to* S.L. *side of the* LION.) Man, what did you get into?

LION. Myself. (*To* DOROTHY.) Little Momma, I almost found that rainbow!

ROYAL GATEKEEPER. (*Entering from the Gate* U.C., *between the* LION *and* TINMAN. *He is haughty, officious, and arrogant.*) Excuse me! But would you mind carrying on in front of another city? (LION *crosses* S.R. *to* R. *of* DOROTHY.)

SCARECROW. (*Crosses* D.S. *to level with* GATEKEEPER.) Who are you?

GATEKEEPER. I am the Royal Gatekeeper. (*Examining* TINMAN.) And we don't allow any . . . (GATEKEEPER *hits* TINMAN's *chest two times with his key.*) trash here in the Big Green Apple.

DOROTHY. (*Crossing* D.S. *of* SCARECROW *to* GATEKEEPER.) But we gotta see the Wiz!

GATEKEEPER. You must be mad! (*Crossing away* S.L., D.S. *of* TINMAN.) The Wiz never sees anyone . . . (*Turning counterclockwise and back in* D.S. *of* TINMAN *and to* S.L. *of*

DOROTHY.) . . . anywhere, or at any time. On the other hand, if you'd care to make it worth my while . . .

TINMAN. Oh, sure. Is it worth it to keep your . . . (TINMAN *takes a swipe at* GATEKEEPER *with his axe.*) kneebone connected to your shinbone? (TINMAN *takes another swipe with axe, and backs the* GATEKEEPER *all the way to* D.R.)

GATEKEEPER. (*All elegance stripped away, becomes funky and "down-home."*) Alright!! Now don't get no attitude!!

TINMAN. (*Crossing back to Gate, and to the* S.L. *end of the group, threatening the scrim with his axe.*) You better let us in, or I'm gonna chop down this gate.

GATEKEEPER. (*Starts to cross in to group, pulling four pairs of green eyeglass frames from inside of the cape he is wearing.*) Oh, very well. But first you have to put on these green glasses. (*He hands them out, giving the three pairs to the* LION, DOROTHY *and* SCARECROW, *and the last pair to* TINMAN *who will put them on upon receipt.*)

SCARECROW. Why? (*Takes glasses.*)

GATEKEEPER. Why? Because that's the rule, that's why. Now begone. (SCARECROW, DOROTHY, *and* LION *exit in that order, through gate, and then turn to* S.R., *exiting* R-2, *before the gate scrim flies out.*)

TINMAN. (*Who has lagged behind, still miffed at the* GATEKEEPER.) I ought to chop down this old gate anyway!

GATEKEEPER. I said: Begone!! (TINMAN *exits through gate, also turns* S.R., *and exits* R-2.) Well, there goes the neighborhood. (GATEKEEPER *also follows the others through the gate, and exits* R-2.)

MUSIC #16: *"EMERALD CITY BALLET"*

(*As the scene bleeds through the scrim, and the scrim finally rises, we see the futuristic Emerald City in all its glory. The* CITIZENS *are exquisitely and exotically dressed, all with green glasses as part of their headdresses. They are Beautiful People, very much aware of it, and as such, are haughty and proud. Their ballet says just this. The following dialogue takes place during the dance by Emerald City Citizens.*)

CITIZENS.
Ahhh.
Please.

Ahhh.
Ahhh.
Ahhh.
Ha! Ha! Ha!
Ssss.
Please.
Ha ha ha ha
Buzz-buzz Buzz-buzz
Do do do/do do do/do do!

(DOROTHY *and her* FRIENDS *enter* R-1.)

DOROTHY. (*Crossing to* FIRST CITIZEN *at* D.C.) Which way to the Wiz? (*All the* CITIZENS *scream with laughter at this question. The laugh goes on until the* LION *in great frustration stops it.*)

LION. (*A great roar.*) Alright!! (*Complete silence from all, as they look at* LION. LION *is cowed by the response, and almost as an apology says . . .*) What's so funny?

FIRST CITIZEN. (*Who is* R.C., *on the second step, crosses* D.S. *and to the* S.R. *side of the* LION.) Nobody sees the Wiz!!

SCARECROW. (L. *of* C. *with* TINMAN.) Why not?

SECOND CITIZEN. (D.L.C., S.L. *of* TINMAN, *crosses* R. *to him.*) They say he's too terrible to behold!!

TINMAN. (*To* SECOND CITIZEN.) What's he look like?

SECOND CITIZEN. (*Crossing away* S.L., *enjoying playing with these naive people.*) A giant Vulture!! (*Does "vulture" pose.*)

THIRD CITIZEN. (U.R.C. *on steps.*) A man-eating elephant!!

FOURTH CITIZEN. (*From* R.C., *crosses* D.S. *between* FIRST CITIZEN *and* LION.) A nine-foot dragon!

(FOURTH CITIZEN *crosses* D.S. FIRST CITIZEN, *toward* S.R., *and then back to position* U.R.C. *All* CITIZENS *laugh uproariously, but the* FIRST CITIZEN, *whose laugh is highly abrasive, laughs longest. Her laugh carries her* D.S. *of the* FOUR FRIENDS *to* D.L.C., *and then back again to* S.R. *of* DOROTHY.)

FIRST CITIZEN. And you . . . (*Touches* DOROTHY'S *white dress . . . definitely out of style in the environment of Emerald City.*) . . . eecch! You want to see the Wiz? (*Screams with laughter again, bending in convulsions, and sees* DOROTHY'S *shoes. Her mood changes abruptly, and she lets out a blood-curdling scream. All other* CITIZENS *freeze and look to where the* FIRST CITIZEN *is pointing.*)

ALL CITIZENS. The Silver Slippers . . . of The Wicked Witch . . . of The East!!!

FIRST CITIZEN. If you wanna see the Wiz, honey, you go right ahead!! (*All the* CITIZENS *exit by the closest way,* L. *and* R., *and in great fear for their lives. The* TINMAN *follows the group exiting toward* S.L., *ending up* L.C.; *the* SCARECROW *does the same with the group* S.R., *leaving* DOROTHY *and the* LION *at approximately* C., *with* DOROTHY *on the* S.L. *side of* LION.)

ACT ONE

SCENE 8

The WIZ's *throne room, the next instant.*

Alone, DOROTHY *and her* FRIENDS *gather their courage to meet the* WIZ.

LION. (*In reference to the departed* CITIZENS.) Fool around with me, will you?

TINMAN. I guess we can go in. (*After line, he crosses* S.R. *to the* S.R. *side of* SCARECROW.)

SCARECROW. I guess so.

DOROTHY. Well . . . here goes!

MUSIC #16A: *FIVE CHORDS*

(*On the fourth chord, a giant spider flies up from* U.L., *terrifying the* FOUR FRIENDS, *who retreat quickly to* D.R.)

DOROTHY. Mr. Wiz!

MUSIC #17 *"SO YOU WANTED TO MEET THE WIZARD"*

(*Before the terrified eyes of* DOROTHY *and the others, two giant doors slide apart, revealing a mask. The mask then flies diagonally toward* S.L., *revealing yet another aperture, not unlike an iris. As this aperture opens, mountains of smoke pour out, and through it, riding on what appears to be a giant tongue, comes the figure of the* WIZ *himself. The* WIZ *moves forward a bit, and when the tongue has reached its final position* D.S., *the* WIZ *strikes a pose, flips his cape open, and he is, indeed, an awe-*

some figure to behold. As he sings, lights flash, and fire springs from hidden sources, thoroughly scaring DOROTHY *and her* FRIENDS.)

WIZ.
SO YOU WANTED TO MEET
　　(WIZ *steps off tongue.*)
THE WIZARD
LET ME TELL YOU THAT YOU'VE COME TO THE
　　RIGHT PLACE
SHALL I MAKE YOU A FROG OR A LIZARD?
　　(*High-pitched laugh—echo.*)
YOU SHOULD SEE THE STRANGE EXPRESSION ON
　　YOUR FACE
　　(WIZ *crosses* S.R., *causing* DOROTHY, SCARECROW, *and* TINMAN *to run* U.S. *of him to* S.L., *as* WIZ *cuts off* LION'S *progress as he tries to follow, trapping him* D.R.)

IF THE WAY I COME ON IS FRIGHTENING
THAT'S THE WAY I FELT LIKE COMING ON
　　TODAY
　　(*Spins to* D.C.)
HAVE YOU EVER BEEN KISSED BY LIGHTNING?
LET ME TELL YOU THAT WILL MAKE YOU GO
　　AWAY!
　　(WIZ *crosses* S.R., *then up the steps to the top platform. As soon as the* LION *has a clear path, he crawls as fast as possible to* S.L. *to rejoin the others, ending up on the* S.R. *side of the* TINMAN, *with* DOROTHY *now* S.L. *of the* TINMAN, *and* SCARECROW S.L. *of* DOROTHY.)

I FLY, AND THE MAGIC OF MY POWER TAKES ME
　　HIGHER
TO A LEVEL WHERE THE CLOUDS TURN INTO FIRE
　　(*Flash bulbs go off* U.S. *of* WIZ.)
IN THE WARMNESS OF THE FIRE
　　(WIZ *crosses* S.L. *end of top platform.*)
I FEEL FINE
　　(*Fire pot goes off under* WIZ.)

JUST KEEP YOUR EYES OPEN AND THE
　　(WIZ *crosses* D.S. *off steps toward* FOUR FRIENDS.)
MAGIC YOU WILL SEE

IT WILL WHISTLE ON THE WIND
AS IT EMANATES FROM ME
IT'S A STRONG AND TRUE VIBRATION,
YOU CAN FEEL IT ON YOUR SKIN
    (WIZ *crosses* D.C.)
NOW COME AND TAKE MY HAND
AND WE WILL DANCE UPON THE WIND
    (FOUR FRIENDS *run* U.S. *of* WIZ *to* D.R.)
NA NA NA NA
    (WIZ *crosses* U.C. *to the top platform where he is also underlit with red, making him look as though he is standing in a bed of fire.*)
SO YOU WANTED TO MEET THE WIZARD!!
    (*On the musical button, he sits on the tongue, and the smoke dies away.*)

WIZ. (*Rises.*) Alright. Who are you?

DOROTHY. Please, Mr. Wiz. (DOROTHY *crosses* L. *toward the* WIZ.)

LION. (*Whispers.*) Dorothy!!

DOROTHY. (*Signals to* LION *that it's okay.*) My name is Dorothy, and this is the Scarecrow, and the Tinman, and the Lion. (*As each is mentioned, they react: The* TINMAN *steps in, the* SCARECROW *waves, and the* LION *curtseys.*)

WIZ. And what do you all want? (*They all advance on the* WIZ, *each answering simultaneously, so we hear nothing but a garble of:*)

DOROTHY. You see, I want to get back to Kansas . . .

LION. Courage, that's what I came after, courage . . .

SCARECROW. You have a set of used brains lying around . . .

WIZ. (*Cutting them off.*) Quiet!! (*They all scurry back to* D.R., *and you can hear a pin drop.*) That's better. (*Crosses* D.S.) Now, I will listen to your problems one at a time, beginning with you! (*He is now* D.C., *and singles out* DOROTHY.) Come here! (LION *sinks to all fours, the others recoil.* DOROTHY *musters up her courage, and comes to the* WIZ, *who slowly turns toward her. The* LION *follows, but at a safe distance.* TINMAN *is next to* SCARECROW, O.S. *side.*) Well??

DOROTHY. (*She expects that the* WIZ *will help.*) Oh, please, Mr. Wiz, you just *gotta* help me get back to Kansas.

WIZ. I don't *gotta* do anything. (WIZ *crosses away* S.L., LION *crosses in another step.*) The great Wiz does as he pleases . . . (WIZ *turns back in—very forcefully.*) and no more!!

DOROTHY. (*Crosses in a step to* WIZ.) Oh, no, sir. You don't *gotta* do nothing at all. But would you?

WIZ. (*For the first time, the* WIZ *has noticed* DOROTHY's *shoes.*) Tell me . . . (*He steps in* . . . LION *growls.*) Where did you get such a marvelous pair of silver pumps?

DOROTHY. From the Good Witch of the North.

WIZ. Ah, Addaperle. (*A friend. The* WIZ *tries this tack.*) How would you like to . . . uh . . . (*Crossing* U.S. *of* DOROTHY *to her* S.R. *side, she turns to meet him.*) trade them for a beautiful Emerald Wizard ring? (*He holds out his right hand, which is adorned with two large Emerald rings.*)

DOROTHY. (*Almost caught.*) Ohhhhh. (*Then remembering.*) Oh, I can't. I gotta keep them on 'til I get home. I made a promise.

WIZ. (*Very loud, a step in as he says:*) Break it!!

DOROTHY. (*Retreating* S.L. *three steps.*) But I was taught never to break a promise.

WIZ. (*Annoyed, crosses* S.L. *toward* DOROTHY, *but again trying a softer approach to draw her in.*) You know, I can understand . . . (DOROTHY *backs around and* D.S. *of* WIZ *retreating toward her* FRIENDS S.R.) why a child like you . . . (WIZ *follows after* DOROTHY, *but sees she is terrified, so opens up toward* S.L. *to spin his magic.*) wanting to go to . . . Brazil . . . Mozambique . . . Harlem. (*SUBSTITUTE: in L.A.—COMPTON.* WIZ *turns to* DOROTHY.) But Kansas? Did I hear you correctly? Get back to Kansas?

DOROTHY. (*Crosses* L. *toward* WIZ.) Yessir!

WIZ. (*Again, very loud, and advancing on* DOROTHY, *driving her back* S.R. *toward* LION.) And what's wrong with it here?

DOROTHY. (*A bit cowed.*) Nothin'.

WIZ. Does my fantastic Emerald City displease you?

DOROTHY. Oh, no sir. I think it's the most beautiful place I've ever seen. (*Starts her defense, which is listing all the things the* WIZ *has run away from, and cannot bear to hear. He backs away toward* S.L., *and* DOROTHY *keeps advancing on him, backing all the way to the* L-2 *portal.*) But there's my home. And there's Aunt Em, and Uncle Henry, and Toto, and I can't just forget about them, can I?

WIZ. (*Again, very loud.*) You may do whatever **you** want. (DOROTHY *backs away.*) Besides, what is home . . . (WIZ *advances on* DOROTHY, *with both of them crossing* D.S. *of* LION *who is at* C., *and all the way to* D.R., *where* DOROTHY *bumps into, and is held protectively by* SCARECROW.) but a place you leave anyway . . . full of broken furniture, faded memories, and shattered dreams . . . Why *not* forget it? (LION *growls, advancing on the* WIZ's *back, and* WIZ *suddenly whirls on him.*) Lion!! (LION, *caught in the act, does mime of playing the violin, and sashays* S.L. *on his*

knees, doing the first eight bars of "SWEET GEORGIA BROWN.")
What do you want?

LION. (*Gets up, and cries out.*) To get the hell out of here!!
Heeellllppp!!!

WIZ. (*Laughs—echo. As he crosses* D.S. *of the* LION *heading toward* L.C., *the* LION *stifles his cry for "Help." At the end of the echo, the* WIZ *turns on the* LION *and:*) Is that your only request?

LION. Yes, sir . . . (*The other three friends say "no," and encourage the* LION *to ask for courage.*) and I agree . . . (LION *is torn between his friends encouraging him, and his terror of the* WIZ.) what's a home but broken furniture . . . faded memories . . . cold oatmeal and, oh, (*Sinks to his knees.*) if you only knew my momma!!

WIZ. (*Laughs—echo—crosses in toward the* LION. *Talking as though to a child.*) But, what is it you want?

LION. (*Ashamed.*) Some courage.

WIZ. (*Another laugh—echo.* WIZ *crosses* S.L. *of* LION *to* L. *of* C.) You mean the mighty king of the jungle is a coward. (*The* WIZ *crosses in to the* LION, *and seizes him by the tail. The* LION *falls with his head toward* S.R.)

LION. Only when I'm scared!

WIZ. (*Mocking him.*) Weakness! That's your only strength. (*The* WIZ *crosses* S.R., *then up the steps to* U.R.C. *on the top platform. As* WIZ *moves, the others run to* LION *to comfort him. The* SCARECROW *ends up* D.L.C. *of the steps,* LION *heads under the bridge* U.L., DOROTHY *behind him, and* TINMAN D.S. *of her also* S.L. *The* TINMAN *sets his axe against the door to the Engine room.*) Scarecrow!! Come here!! (*The* SCARECROW *turns to face the* WIZ, *and on his first step, shaking with fright, he falls flat on his face. He then gets up and crosses up the stairs, seated on the third from the top,* D.S. *and slightly* S.L. *of the* WIZ. DOROTHY *moves* D.S. *into the protecting arms of the* TINMAN, *and together they watch the following.*) Are you a coward, too?

SCARECROW. A coward? Oh, no sir. I haven't got the brains to be afraid of anything.

WIZ. Oh, no? (*He causes fire to leap from a firepot directly under where he stands. In great terror, the* SCARECROW *leaps back, ending up* D.L., *again quaking in fear.*)

SCARECROW. Except for fire. I know that much.

WIZ. Not afraid of anything, you thought? How little we know ourselves. (*The* WIZ *slowly crosses down the steps toward the* SCARECROW, *who does a back hinge, finally ending up flat on his back* D.L., *with his head toward the* S.L. *portal leg. The* WIZ's *entire move* D.S. *is done in silence, and he ends up* U.S. *of the* SCARECROW.) Which is more deceptive: the foolish wise man, or the wise fool?

SCARECROW. (*Sitting up.*) The foolish wise man or the wise fool? Don't ask me. I never was any good at multiple choice.

WIZ. (*Picking up* SCARECROW *and throwing him* S.R.) Why, you dumb sack of straw!! (SCARECROW *rolls to* S.R., *then crawls* U.S. *under the* S.R. *end of the* U.C. *platform, cowering. The* WIZ *follows* SCARECROW's *progress, ending up at* C. *The* TINMAN, *knowing he will be summoned next, comforts* DOROTHY *saying that he will be alright.*) Tinman!! (*In a broad gesture, exerting his power over the* TINMAN, *the* WIZ *draws* TINMAN D.S. *to level with him, causing the* TINMAN *to groan as he moves. As soon as the* TINMAN *leaves her,* DOROTHY *crosses* U.S. *to the* LION, *who moves out from under the bridge and sits on the steps far* S.L. *end.* DOROTHY *sits* D.S. *of* LION. *The* WIZ, *using only his index finger, beckons the* TINMAN *to move into a position* S.L. *of him, in five motions, each accompanied by a step in by the* TINMAN, *and also a groan. When the* TINMAN *is next to the* WIZ, *the* WIZ *snaps his head around to freeze the* TINMAN's *progress with a stare. He then opens and shuts his hand twice, causing the* TINMAN *to rock back and forth each time, and finally, points to the floor, causing the* TINMAN *to kneel at his feet. As soon as the* TINMAN's *knee hits the stage floor, the* WIZ *turns and faces him.*) Do you know anything or not?

TINMAN. Only that I want a heart, your Wizness!!

(*A look by* WIZ *to the audience, and then in two great peals of laughter, the* WIZ *crosses* S.R., *all the way to the portal leg. The laugh is re-enforced by echo. The* TINMAN *rises, one quick look to his* FRIENDS, *to determine what could possibly be this funny, and follows after the* WIZ. *As the second peal of laughter ends, the* WIZ *whirls around, and he and the* TINMAN *are nose to nose.*)

WIZ. What on earth for? Without one, you'll never know pain . . . (*The* WIZ *hits* TINMAN's U.S. *shoulder, turning the* TINMAN *around clockwise, and as he does, the* WIZ *moves* U.S. *of* TINMAN, *so that he is on* L. *side of him for* . . .) or hurt˙ . . . (*The* WIZ *gives the* TINMAN *an open-handed karate chop across his chest, almost breaking his hand in the process. After controlling the pain, he turns and faces the* TINMAN *for . . .) or* sorrow. (*The* WIZ *stares the* TINMAN *to his knees and then crosses to* C.)

TINMAN. (*On* D.S. *knee.*) But . . . (*The* WIZ'S *cross to* C. *is stopped here.*) there's more to feeling things than just that, isn't there?

MUSIC #18:   *"IF I COULD FEEL"*

WIZ. Possibly. (*The* WIZ *turns* D.S., *and takes a step back in toward* TINMAN.) But are you sure it's worth the suffering?

TINMAN. Oh, I'll take my chances, your Wizness. (*The* WIZ *disconnects from the* TINMAN, *faces* U.S., *and spreads his cape out behind him in the same pose of impenetrability that we have seen before.*) I'll take my chances.

WHAT WOULD I DO IF I COULD SUDDENLY FEEL
AND KNOW ONCE AGAIN, THAT WHAT I FEEL IS
      REAL
I COULD CRY, I COULD SMILE
I MIGHT LAY BACK FOR A WHILE
TELL ME WHAT, WHAT WOULD I DO
      (TINMAN *rises*)
IF I COULD FEEL?
      (WIZ *crosses* U.S. *to the top platform and sits on the tongue. As he passes by* DOROTHY *and the* LION, *they move quickly toward* S.R., *with* DOROTHY *against the engine room door, and the* LION *on all fours* S.R. *of her.* TINMAN *crosses* D.S. *three steps and continues . . .*)

WHAT WOULD I DO IF I COULD SUDDENLY SEE
AND KNOW WHAT I SAW WASN'T FOOLIN' ME
AND THEN MAYBE AFTER A WHILE I MIGHT SEE A
      BABY SMILE
AND I NOTICE HOW SHE WOULD GRIN AFTER I HAD
      TOUCHED HER CHIN
AND IF A TEAR CAME TO HER EYE
      (*Does very mechanical tear.*)
THINK OF ALL THE WOUNDS THEY'D MEND
AND JUST THINK TO OF THE TIME I COULD
      SPEND
BEING VULNERABLE AGAIN
TELL ME WHAT, WHAT WOULD I DO
WHAT WOULD I DO , WHAT, WHAT WOULD I DO
      (*Crosses* S.L. *to* D.L.C.)

WHAT WOULD I DO
OH, MR. WIZNESS
    (*Turns full circle.*)
IF I COULD FEEL
    (*Crosses* U.S. *up steps toward* WIZ.)
IF I COULD FEEL
    (WIZ's *hand out to* TINMAN, *but then withdraws just before*
    TINMAN *can make contact.* TINMAN *turns* D.S. WIZ *rises.*)
Will you help me get a heart, your Wizness?
    WIZ. Will you lay off the Wizness business? (*He crosses* S.R. *on*
the platform, then down the steps on the S.R. *end. As he passes the*
SCARECROW, *the* SCARECROW, *still terrified from the last exchange,*
gets up and runs back toward his friends. The TINMAN *stops his*
progress with a comforting arm around his waist.) Come now, I
have made my decision. (*All four give their attention to the* WIZ.
DOROTHY *and the* LION *cross* D.S. *enough to establish contact. To*
the TINMAN . . .) I will give you a heart . . . (TINMAN *crosses in*
step, and ad libs joy. To the SCARECROW . . .) And I will get you
some brains . . . (SCARECROW *crosses in to* TINMAN, *and ad libs*
joy. To the LION. . .) and you, courage . . . (LION *and* DOROTHY
cross in to TINMAN *and* SCARECROW, *as* LION *also ad libs joy* . . .)
And I will get Dorothy back to Kansas . . . (*This is the topper, all*
are ecstatic, and rush S.R. *toward the* WIZ *to thank him. Just as*
DOROTHY, *who is first in line to get to him arrives, the* WIZ *holds up*
his hand and roars . . .) If!!!!
    DOROTHY. (*Apprehensive.*) If what??
    WIZ. (*Said to* DOROTHY, *backing her and the whole line of*
FRIENDS, *who are in order:* TINMAN, SCARECROW, *and* LION *bring-*
ing up the rear.) If you kill . . . the most evil . . . the most
wicked . . . the most powerful of all the witches in Oz . . . The
Wicked Witch of the West.
    DOROTHY. But I couldn't do something like that!!
    WIZ. Why not? You've already killed one wicked witch.
    DOROTHY. But that was an accident!!
    WIZ. (*Really loud.*) I do not care how it happened. (*Crosses* D.R.;
softer, an objective evaluation.) You're the best wicked witch killer
in this country. (WIZ *remains facing* D.R.)
    SCARECROW. (*Off the wall question, as though not paying any*
attention to what is going on, SCARECROW *crosses* S.R. *to right*
behind the WIZ. *As he breaks for this move,* TINMAN *gets* DOROTHY
seated on the second step from the bottom, L.C. *of the step unit.*) Mr.
Wiz, what do *I* have to do to get my brains?
    WIZ. (*Turning slowly to the* SCARECROW, *astounded that anyone*

could be so stupid.) Kill The Wicked Witch of the West, of course. (WIZ *seizes* SCARECROW *by his lapels, and flings him back toward* S.L. *The* LION *steps* D.S. *to stop* SCARECROW'S *backward progress, and to keep him from falling.*)

SCARECROW. You just told Dorothy that *she* had to do that!!

WIZ. (*Crossing in to* SCARECROW *at* C. . . . *and as he moves in, the* LION *moves away quickly toward* S.L.) It does not matter who does it. This is a package deal. (WIZ *crosses* U.S. *to level* DOROTHY.) As long as the Wicked Witch of the West still lives, none of you gets anything!! (WIZ *starts to exit up the stairs to* U.C. DOROTHY *grabs the* D.S. *edge of his cape.*)

DOROTHY. But I don't want to go around killing nobody!

WIZ. Dorothy . . . (*Removing cape from her hand.*) if you want to get back to Kansas bad enough, you're just going to have to pay for it!

DOROTHY. But, Mr. Wiz . . .

WIZ. (*Really loud, with full echo.*) NOOOOOOO!!!! (*The* FOUR FRIENDS *reel back, as though in a great wind storm.*) I have spoken!!

MUSIC #19: "*SO YOU WANTED TO MEET THE WIZARD*"

(*Smoke again pours out of the tongue, as the* WIZ *crosses* U.S., *mounts it, and the iris opens fully, allowing him to pass through, and then closes behind him. The* TINMAN *holds* DOROTHY, *the* SCARECROW, *who is* S.L. *of* TINMAN, *still waves in the breeze, and the* LION *faints as* . . .)

CURTAIN, ACT ONE

ACT TWO

Scene 1

The castle of the Wicked Witch of the West (Evillene). *A few days later.*

MUSIC IN: *"WINKIE CHANT"*

(In the dreadful palace of the Wicked Witch of the West, *slave-like* Winkies *pull and tug on a long rope, at the end of which is something we don't yet see. The* Lord High Underling, *a weak coward of a man, and a bully, and a toady for* Evillene, *beats and whips the* Winkies *as they cross. Entering* R-2 *Entrance and crossing to* L-2 *Exit. Through this he shouts:)*

Lord High Underling. Make way! Make way! Make way for the Wicked Witch of the West! Make way for . . . *Evillene!*

(The Winkies *pull and tug and moan and cry, and now we see they are pulling* Evillene's *massive rolling throne on stage. It's cold and ugly and hung with carcasses.* Evillene *herself is low-down evil. One just knows there isn't a kind bone in her imposing body or a good thought in her rotten mind. She tolerates the moaning and crying of the* Winkies *for just so long, [but not before the throne has settled at* D.L.C.] *and then:)*

Evillene. Shut up! *(Music and chant out.)* 'Cause I'm evil with everyone today!

MUSIC #21: *"NO BAD NEWS"*

WHEN I WAKE UP IN THE MORNING
WHICH IT PLEASES ME TO DO
DON'T NOBODY BRING ME NO BAD NEWS
'CAUSE I WAKE UP ALREADY NEGATIVE
AND I'VE WIRED UP MY FUSE
SO DON'T NOBODY BRING ME NO BAD NEWS,
    (Rises, crosses to R.C.)

IF WE'RE GOIN' TO BE BUDDIES
BETTER BONE UP ON THE RULES
'CAUSE DON'T NOBODY BRING ME NO BAD NEWS
YOU CAN BE MY BEST OF FRIENDS
AS OPPOSED TO PAYIN' DUES
    (*Hits* WINKIE *with skirt.*)
CUZ DON'T NOBODY BRING ME
NO BAD NEWS
    (*Crosses* D.L.)

NO BAD NEWS
NO BAD NEWS
DON'T NOBODY BRING ME NO BAD NEWS
'CAUSE I'LL MAKE YOU AN OFFER, CHILD
THAT YOU CANNOT REFUSE
    (*Spoken.*) Get that one!
'CAUSE DON'T NOBODY BRING ME NO BAD NEWS
    (*Crosses* U.S. *to throne.*)

WHEN YOU'RE TALKIN' TO ME
DON'T BE CRYIN' THE BLUES 'CAUSE
DON'T NOBODY BRING ME NO BAD NEWS
YOU CAN VERBALIZE AND VOCALIZE
BUT JUST GIVE ME THE CLUES 'CAUSE
DON'T NOBODY BRING ME NO BAD NEWS

BRING THE MESSAGE IN YOUR HEAD
OR IN SOMETHING YOU CAN'T LOSE
CUZ DON'T NOBODY BRING ME NO BAD NEWS
    (*Kicks* WINKIE.)
IF YOU'RE GONNA BRING ME SOMETHING
BRING ME SOMETHING I CAN USE
CUZ DON'T NOBODY BRING ME NO BAD NEWS
    (*She sits on the throne which is moved by the* WINKIES *to* D.L.)

NO BAD NEWS,
NO BAD NEWS
DON'T NOBODY BRING ME NO BAD NEWS
BETTER WATCH THE WAY YOU
PLACE THE WORDS, THAT YOU
MIGHT CHANCE TO CHOOSE
CUZ DON'T NOBODY BRING ME

NO BAD NEWS
NO BAD NEWS
NO BAD NEWS
DON'T NOBODY BRING ME NO BAD NEWS
BECAUSE I'LL MAKE YOU AN OFFER CHILD
    (*Throne is moved by* WINKIES *to* D.R.)
THAT YOU CANNOT REFUSE
'CAUSE DON'T NOBODY BRING ME
    (*Throne is now moved to* U.C.)

DON'T NOBODY BRING ME
DON'T NOBODY BRING ME
DON'T NOBODY BRING ME
DON'T NOBODY BRING ME
DON'T NOBODY BRING ME
DON'T NOBODY BRING ME
NO BAD NEWS!!
    (*Orchestra chord.*)

'Cause I ain't goin' for it!! (*Musical button. All but four of the* WINKIES *leave. Three of the four who stay behind will move the throne during the rest of the scene. The fourth is the* LORD HIGH UNDERLING, *who is* U.R. *in the shadows.*) Now where is that Lord High Underling?

LORD HIGH UNDERLING. (*Very obsequious, he crosses to the* S.R. *side of the throne.*) You summoned me, oh Beautiful Mistress?

EVILLENE. Well, what's the situation with Dorothy?

LORD HIGH UNDERLING. I should have news from the front at any moment now. Good news. (*He laughs.*)

EVILLENE. (*For the first time, she notices he is standing as he speaks to her.*) On your knees when you speak to me. (*He instantly drops to his knees, grovelling.* EVILLENE *starts pulling up her skirt.*) Now kiss my . . . (*A red-booted foot pops out from under* EVILLENE's *skirt.*) foot! (*He kisses it once. The smell is awful, and he recoils in disgust.*) Oooo! One more time. A little higher, and about an inch to the right. (*He kisses her foot again, and again . . . and as he does, the* WINKIES *behind the throne pull* EVILLENE *and the throne toward* L.C. EVILLENE *is in an ecstasy all her own.*) It's so good to be a liberated woman.

(TWO WINKIES *drag in a terrified* MESSENGER, *flinging him on his knees toward* EVILLENE's *throne. The* LORD HIGH UNDERLING, *now that the heat is off him, rises and starts beating the* WINKIES *who are* U.S. *of the throne.*)

FIRST WINKIE. (*Who has entered from* R-2, *with* MESSENGER.) Oh, Most Wicked Majesty . . . the messenger has arrived.

(*The* TWO WINKIES *exit* R-2, *leaving the terrified* MESSENGER L. *of* C., *shaking.*)

MESSENGER. A message, your Evilness.

EVILLENE. Oh, yeah?

MESSENGER. Yeah.

EVILLENE. Well, for your sake, it had better be *good* news.

MESSENGER. (*Lying. Trying to save himself.*) Oh, yeah. I got a really good piece of good news for you . . . mostly.

EVILLENE. *Mostly?*

MESSENGER. Yeah!

EVILLENE. What do you mean: Mostly?

MESSENGER. Well, firstly, Dorothy and her friends are still on their way up here, and they're gonna do you in . . . (*He points at her on "do you in" as she will then be off his back also.*)

EVILLENE. What? (*She breaks up in laughter at such an incredible idea. Seeing her laugh, the* LORD HIGH UNDERLING, *now at the* S.L. *side of the throne, also breaks up laughing, and starts beating the* WINKIES *to get them laughing.* EVILLENE *finally becomes aware of their laughter, and not being one to allow such luxury, even on a false premise, bellows* . . .) Shut up!! (*Instant silence. As* EVILLENE'S *attention is drawn back to the* MESSENGER, *the* LORD HIGH UNDERLING *starts blessing himself, just in case her wrath is directed at him.*)

MESSENGER. Secondly, we couldn't get the silver slippers away from Dorothy.

EVILLENE. (*Even angrier.*) What?

MESSENGER. And thirdly, I gotta go now!! (*He crawls away to* R.C., *but* EVILLENE *rises from her throne and crosses after him to about* D.C.)

EVILLENE. (*Crossing on the line.*) But you've brought me nothing but *bad* news. Where's the *good* news you promised?

MESSENGER. (*Maybe she'll buy it long enough for him to get out the door.*) The good news is . . . there ain't no more bad news.

(*He starts to crawl toward the* R-1 *exit, but* EVILLENE *is in hot pursuit, and steps on his robe, fastening him to the deck.*)

EVILLENE. (*Whirling on the* LORD HIGH UNDERLING.) Who hired this jive turkey?

LORD HIGH UNDERLING. (*Crossing in,* D.S. *of the throne.*) Well, I did. Why?

EVILLENE. Well, a pox on your house!

LORD HIGH UNDERLING. A pox on *my* house?

EVILLENE. (*With a sweeping gesture taking in the* MESSENGER.) A pox on *both* your houses!

LORD HIGH UNDERLING. (*In tears.*) My summer place, too?

EVILLENE. Oh, shut up! (*The* MESSENGER *now tries to sneak away toward the* R-1 *exit, while* EVILLENE'*s attention is on the* LORD HIGH UNDERLING. *Just as he gets to the exit,* EVILLENE *turns and sees him.*) Come back here, you! (*She does three long voodoo chants, drawing him back toward her by witchcraft. He crawls in place, exerting great effort, but makes no headway. Finally he is moving backwards, and although fighting against it, ends up directly* D.S. *of* EVILLENE, *still on his knees, and with her hands on either side of his face. He shakes uncontrallably, and cries in terror.*) Now, now, now, I know it's not your fault.

MESSENGER. (*Crying through . . .*) No, it's not my fault . . .

EVILLENE. . . . So I'm going to be very fair about this . . .

MESSENGER. (*Suddenly hopeful. He may make it after all.*) Very fair . . . Good! I can leave. (*On his knees, he crawls toward the* R-2 *exit.*)

EVILLENE. (*Exploding.*) Hang that sucker! (TWO WINKIES *from behind the throne run toward* S.R., *to seize the* MESSENGER *as he dives for* EVILLENE'*s feet to beg for mercy.*)

MESSENGER. No, Evillene. Don't hang me!! (*He continues as* WINKIES *drag him out* R-2.) No, no, no, please! Don't hang me. Let me go! Nooo!

EVILLENE. (*Boiling mad. She has done all her goodness, expired all her compassion for the month. She crosses* D.R.) All right!! (*She opens two huge eyes on the ends of each of her ample breasts. The eyes are white, with black dots for pupils.*) I'm through being Mr. Nice Guy. (*She hooks her thumbs into two rings, and makes the eyelids blink two or three times.*) I'm going to summon my Winged Monkey!!

LORD HIGH UNDERLING. (*Still* S.L. *of the throne where he re-*

treated after his last interchange with EVILLENE, *and blessing him-self. Now, he crosses* D.S. *of the throne for:*) Oh, no!
EVILLENE. Oh, yeah!!
LORD HIGH UNDERLING. Not the Winged Monkey!!

(*He runs* U.S. *of the throne where he will help the remaining* WINKIE *move and finally strike the throne.* EVILLENE *does a black magic voodoo chant from* D.R., *which also has a choral backing by the* PIT SINGERS. *The lights change, and make her chamber even eerier. Finally, the* LEADER OF THE WINGED MONKEYS *leaps on stage, uttering a karate attack scream. He is an evil, surly fellow, not in awe of* EVILLENE *or anyone else for that matter. He is the "hit" man for the syndicate. During* EVILLENE'S *chant, the remaining* WINKIE *and the* LORD HIGH UNDERLING *have moved the throne in circular movements, as though it has been levitating as a result of the chant. The throne must be* U.L. *for the* MONKEY'S *entrance, and stopped moving. The* MONKEY *enters from* L-1, *doing karate attack exercises, and screaming all the way. He ends with a violent punch and scream, composes himself, and gets into a* MONKEY *crouch, with one hand on the deck.*)

MONKEY. Okay, baby! I'm here. But it's not because of you. It's because of that dumb chant.
EVILLENE. (*Crossing* U.S. *of* MONKEY *heading for her throne.*) Don't you come signifying to me, you little ape, or I'll put a spell on your . . . coconuts. (*The* MONKEY, *just in case, does a flying leap and roll to* D.R. EVILLENE *sits on her throne* U.L.C.)
MONKEY. So what are you going to lay on me and the gang this time?
EVILLENE. Something right up your alley. (*The* MONKEY *moves in to sit just beneath and* S.R. *of* EVILLENE *in three moves across stage.*) A couple of cats who need straightening out.
MONKEY. Gottcha!! Who?
EVILLENE. A scarecrow, a Tinman, a Lion, and a little . . . (*Rolled* R.) . . . brat named Dorothy. (*Spits in hate.*)
MONKEY. (*Gets up, spins, laughs hysterically.*) A scarecrow, a Tinman, a Lion, and a little brat named Dorothy. (*Laughs again.*) You don't get along with nobody, do you?
EVILLENE. Oh, shut up! (MONKEY *leaps back to* C.) And do as I command, and bring them here. (MONKEY *starts to prepare for the task. He hyperventilates, and summons up all his hatred.*) When I

get my hands on Dorothy's silver slippers . . . all of Oz will kiss my feet! (*The remaining* WINKIE *and the* LORD HIGH UNDERLING *drag the throne off* L-1. EVILLENE *laughs through the exit.*)

ACT TWO

SCENE 2

MUSIC #22: "FUNKY MONKEYS"

(*This dance depicts the treachery of the* WINGED MONKEYS *as a mob, and the capture and kidnapping of* DOROTHY *and her* FRIENDS. *During dance.*)

EVILLENE. All of Oz will be mine!

(*Near end of dance.* LION *enters* R-1 *with* DOROTHY *in arms.* SCARECROW *and* TINMAN *enter* R-1. *Friends captured.*)

ACT TWO

SCENE 3

EVILLENE'S *Palace, about a week later.*

Misery continues, as we see THREE WINKIES *crossing from* S.L. *to* S.R., *carrying huge sacks full of a heavy but unknown substance. The* LORD HIGH UNDERLING *is whipping them as they pass.*

Finally, when all the WINKIES *have disappeared* O.R., *the* LION *enters* R-2 *carrying two water buckets.*

LORD HIGH UNDERLING. (*Attacking* LION *with his whip.*) You, too, Lion. Move along there.

(*The* LION *exits* L-2, *followed by the* LORD HIGH UNDERLING. *As soon as he is off,* DOROTHY *backs on from* R-1. *She wears an apron, and has obviously been doing heavy domestic work.*

LION *re-enters from* L-2, *and seeing* DOROTHY, *crosses in to* L.C., *puts the buckets down.*)

LION. Dorothy!
DOROTHY. Lion! (*She runs to his arms and they embrace.*)
LION. Are you all right?
DOROTHY. I guess so. What's that old witch got *you* doin'?
LION. (*His back hurts, and she obliges by rubbing and scratching.*) Carrying all the water out of this place.
DOROTHY. They got you carrying water?
LION. Little Momma, she got me feelin' like Gunga Din. Child, you know that lady is so afraid of water, she don't even take a bath? (*He crosses away* S.L. *a bit.*)
DOROTHY. She doesn't?
LION. (*Crossing back to her, a shared secret.*) No . . . She just sends herself out to be dry-cleaned.

(*From Off* R-2, *we hear* EVILLENE'S *laughter, and then she enters, preceded by grovelling* WINKIES. *The* LION *and* DOROTHY *run to* D.R., *as* OTHER WINKIES *come back from Left and Right.*)

EVILLENE. We've got 'em all, and we're gonna have straw soup. (*She crosses to* C., *turns back and sees* DOROTHY *and the* LION D.R.) Well, well, well . . . I don't remember telling anyone to take five!

(ONE *of the* WINKIES *makes a noise with a water bucket left by the* LION *at* L.C. EVILLENE *is noticeably upset by the presence of the water.*)

DOROTHY. Oh, please, Mrs. Witch. I haven't seen the Lion since I've been here.
EVILLENE. (*Crossing to* R. *of* C.) So what? Just get back to work. I want you to scrub the floors, polish the silver, vacuum the rugs . . . and you *do* do windows, don't you? (*Then, to the* LION.) And you! Get that water out of my sight! (DOROTHY *and the* LION *cross hand in hand* U.S. *of* EVILLENE *toward the buckets.* EVILLENE *stops them with: super sweet.*) Dorothy, wait! (*She crosses to* DOROTHY, *who hides behind the* LION *at* L. *of* C.) When are you going to give me those lovely silver slippers?
DOROTHY. I can't.
EVILLENE. (*Tightens—the claw—then relaxes and tries charm one more time.*) I'll give you all . . . (*Crosses* D.S.) . . . my beauty tips.

LION. Oh, lord, Momma, don't nobody want those.

DOROTHY. I'll never take my shoes off.

EVILLENE. *(Exploding, closing in on* DOROTHY *who is still shielded by the* LION.) Give them to me, you little brat!

LION. *(Screwing up his courage.)* Big Momma, do you know what my owl would say about you?

EVILLENE. *(Stopped cold. This may be a compliment.)* Owl? No. What?

LION. You crazy! (LION *quickly retreats to* DOROTHY *at* L.C.)

EVILLENE. Is that a put-down?

LION. No, your Fatness . . . it's just a . . .

EVILLENE. Your *Fatness? (She grabs his right arm, and starts twising it in a hammer lock.)* For that, I'm going to have your hide!

LION. No! I'm an endangered species. *(To* DOROTHY.) Tell her!

(ONE *of the* WINKIES *grabs* DOROTHY *and points to a bucket of water.* DOROTHY *picks up the bucket and throws its contents on the* WICKED WITCH.)

DOROTHY. You leave my lion alone, you . . . you . . . *(As the water hits* EVILLENE, *she cries out in panic. She backs up toward* S.R.)

EVILLENE. Look what you've done. You ruined me! *(She starts to melt.)* Water! The only thing I'm powerless against. The only thing that could destroy me! *(She moves onto the trap.)* Winkies . . . help!! *(She melts into the floor and disappears, as* DOROTHY, *her* FRIENDS, *and the* WINKIES *watch in amazement.)*

DOROTHY. Oh, Lord, don't tell me I've done it again!

(Orchestra Chord.)

WINKIES. Hallelujah!!

LION. *(Holds onto* DOROTHY *at* L.C.) What the hell was that?

ONE WINKIE. Thanks to you, child, we're all free.

MUSIC #24:   *"BRAND NEW DAY"* (Everybody Rejoice.)

WINKIES.
HALLELUJAH!! HALLELUJAH!
WOMAN.
EVERYBODY LOOK AROUND
'CAUSE THERE'S A REASON TO REJOICE, YOU SEE

Two Women.
EVERYBODY COME OUT
AND LET'S COMMENCE TO SINGING JOYFULLY
  Two Women and One Man
EVERYBODY LOOK UP
AND FIND THE HOPE THAT WE'VE BEEN WAITING ON
  Two Women, Two Men.
EVERYBODY BE GLAD
BECAUSE OUR SILENT FEAR AND DREAD IS GONE
    (DOROTHY *and* LION *exit* L-1.)
  All Winkies.
FREEDOM, YOU SEE
HAS GOT OUR HEARTS SINGING SO JOYFULLY
LOOK ABOUT
YOU OWE IT TO YOURSELF TO CHECK IT OUT
CAN'T YOU FEEL A BRAND NEW DAY?
CAN'T YOU FEEL A BRAND NEW DAY?
CAN'T YOU FEEL A BRAND NEW DAY?
CAN'T YOU FEEL A BRAND NEW DAY?
    (*Dance extension. Through the number, the* WINKIES *become
    free people.*)
  Woman.
EVERYBODY BE GLAD
BECAUSE THE SUN IS SHINING JUST FOR US
  Two Women.
EVERYBODY WAKE UP, INTO THE MORNING
INTO HAPPINESS
  All.
HELLO WORLD
  Two Women.
IT'S LIKE A DIFFERENT WAY OF LIVING NOW
  All.
THANK YOU, WORLD
  Two Men.
WE ALWAYS KNEW THAT WE'D BE FREE SOMEHOW
  Girls.
IN HARMONY
LET'S SHOW THE WORLD THAT WE'VE GOT LIBERTY
  Men.
IT'S SUCH A CHANGE
FOR US TO LIVE SO INDEPENDENTLY

GIRLS.
FREEDOM, YOU SEE,
HAS GOT OUR HEARTS SINGING SO JOYFULLY
ALL.
JUST LOOK ABOUT
YOU OWE IT TO YOURSELF TO CHECK IT OUT

CAN'T YOU FEEL A BRAND NEW DAY?
CAN'T YOU FEEL A BRAND NEW DAY?
    (*Dance extension.*)
DOROTHY.
EVERYBODY BE GLAD
BECAUSE THE SUN IS SHINING JUST FOR US
EVERYBODY WAKE UP
INTO THE MORNING, INTO HAPPINESS

HELLO, WORLD
IT'S LIKE A DIFFERENT WAY OF LIVING NOW
THANK YOU, WORLD
WE ALWAYS KNEW THAT WE'D BE FREE SOMEHOW
ALL.
IN HARMONY
LET'S SHOW THE WORLD THAT WE'VE GOT LIBERTY
IT'S SUCH A CHANGE
FOR US TO LIVE SO INDEPENDENTLY
FREEDOM, YOU SEE
HAS GOT OUR HEARTS SINGING SO JOYFULLY
JUST LOOK ABOUT
YOU OWE IT TO YOURSELF TO CHECK IT OUT

CAN'T YOU FEEL A BRAND NEW DAY?
CAN'T YOU FEEL A BRAND NEW DAY?
CAN'T YOU FEEL A BRAND NEW DAY?
CAN'T YOU FEEL A BRAND NEW DAY?
CAN'T YOU FEEL A BRAND NEW DAY?
CAN'T YOU FEEL A BRAND NEW DAY?
CAN'T YOU FEEL A BRAND NEW DAY?
CAN'T YOU FEEL A BRAND NEW DAY?
    (DOROTHY *and her* FRIENDS *wave goodbye and exit* R-1. *Dance extension.*)

EVERYBODY BE GLAD
BECAUSE THE SUN IS SHINING JUST FOR US

EVERYBODY WAKE UP
INTO THE MORNING, INTO HAPPINESS

HELLO, WORLD
IT'S LIKE A DIFFERENT WAY OF LIVING NOW
THANK YOU, WORLD,
WE ALWAYS KNEW THAT WE'D BE FREE SOMEHOW

IN HARMONY
LET'S SHOW THE WORLD THAT WE'VE GOT LIBERTY

IT'S SUCH A CHANGE
FOR US TO LIVE SO INDEPENDENTLY

FREEDOM, YOU SEE
HAS GOT OUR HEARTS SINGING SO JOYFULLY

JUST LOOK ABOUT
YOU OWE IT TO YOURSELF TO CHECK IT OUT

CAN'T YOU FEEL A BRAND NEW DAY?
CAN'T YOU FEEL A BRAND NEW DAY?
CAN'T YOU FEEL A BRAND NEW DAY?
CAN'T YOU FEEL A BRAND NEW DAY?
CAN'T YOU FEEL A BRAND NEW DAY?
CAN'T YOU FEEL A BRAND NEW DAY?
CAN'T YOU FEEL A BRAND NEW DAY?
CAN'T YOU FEEL A BRAND NEW DAY?

ACT TWO

SCENE 4

In front of the gates to Emerald City, a morning some time later.

The ROYAL GATEKEEPER *enters through the gate, singing to himself . . . an aria, or at least the warm-up to one. He is having a grand time.*

GATEKEEPER. (*Suddenly seeing the* FRIENDS *returning Off* R-1.) That bunch is coming back from seeing the Wicked Witch of the West. (*Crosses* S.L. *to* L.C., *false confidence*.) Well, the Wiz gave orders they were never gonna be allowed in the City again, so they can just . . . (*A thought hits him, he stops, and then crosses back toward* C.) *Back* from seeing the Wicked Witch of the West: Alive!! (*He puts two and two together*.) That means that she must be . . . (*He crosses* S.L.) And if they did that to her . . . (*He stops in his tracks*.) and I tell them that they can't . . . Oh! I wish I was back on unemployment!

(*He puts his cape over his head and exits through the gate, and toward* S.R., *remaining* U.S. *of the scrim*. DOROTHY *and her Friends enter* R-1, *all singing "BRAND NEW DAY." The* TINMAN *enters first, and crosses to the* S.L. *side of the gate opening. The* SCARECROW *and* DOROTHY *enter next,* DOROTHY *on the* D.S. *side, arm in arm, and cross* D.S. *of* TINMAN *to* L.C., *with scarecrow on the onstage side of* DOROTHY *when in position. The* LION *enters last, and crosses to* R. *of* C.)

TINMAN. (*Knocks with handle of axe on deck: "shave and a haircut . . . two bits." Then he sings out:*)
HELLO, IN THERE!
GATEKEEPER. (*He sings his answer from inside*.)
GOODBYE OUT THERE!
SCARECROW. (*He also sings—operatic*.)
OPEN UP IN THERE!
        (*He crosses in toward the gate*.)
GATEKEEPER. (*Spoken*.) What for? (DOROTHY *crosses in to* S.L. *of* SCARECROW, *and* TINMAN *counters to the* S.L. *side of* DOROTHY.)
LION. (*Like Louis Armstrong, he sings and crosses in to the* S.R. *side of the gate*.)
BECAUSE WE WANT TO SEE THE WIZARD AGAIN, BIG
        DUMMY!
GATEKEEPER. Impossible. He moved!
TINMAN. (*Crosses* D.S. *and in to almost* D.S. *of* DOROTHY.) He *moved?* How come? (DOROTHY *steps* D.S. *to* TINMAN *as he puts his arm around her*.)
GATEKEEPER. I don't know. It had something to do with an urban renewal.
LION. (*Crosses in to* D.S. *of the gate, ready to get rough about it*.

As he moves in, SCARECROW *counters to* S.R. *side of the gate.*) You better urban this gate.

GATEKEEPER. I can't. You see, the man with the keys went on vacation until the middle of next month.

LION. (*Explodes in frustration.*) You tell him to take his vacation . . . (*The* SCARECROW *signals the* LION *to cool it, and that he has an idea that will work.*) some other time.

SCARECROW. (*He crosses in to* D.S. *of the gate, so the* GATE-KEEPER *will be sure to hear every word. As he does, the* LION *counters to the* S.R. *side of the gate.*) Well, then, I guess we'd better leave the money and go.

GATEKEEPER. (*Undercut . . . very interested.*) Money? What money?

SCARECROW. (*Letting the others in on his plan, really playing it up.*) Well, we brought back this big bag of loot for the Wiz. How much do you think is in here, Brother Lion? (DOROTHY *giggles, and opens* S.L. *a bit.*)

LION. (*Doesn't get it yet.*) Bag? What bag? (*Finally the dawn. Does real down home moment, like Amos and Andy.*) Well, between the gold and the silver, alone, I'd say somewhere in the vicinity of a round figure . . .

TINMAN. I think there's at least *twice* that much! (*After line,* TINMAN *crosses* S.L. *to enjoy laugh with* DOROTHY.)

SCARECROW. So when the man with the keys comes back . . . the money will be right here by the mail chute. (SCARECROW *reaches his hand out for* DOROTHY *who crosses* D.S. *of* TINMAN *and takes it.*) Come on, Dorothy. We gotta be going before it gets dark.

(*In a line, from* S.R. *to* S.L., *the* LION, SCARECROW, DOROTHY *and* TINMAN *take four overly loud . . . so the* GATEKEEPER *will hear . . . steps toward* R.C., *and then scurry silently* U.S., *so that the* LION *is on the* S.R. *side of the gate, the* SCARECROW *on the* S.L. *side, with* DOROTHY *next to him, and* TINMAN *on the far* S.L. *side. The* GATEKEEPER *enters giggling to himself that he is about to make a coup.*)

GATEKEEPER. Gold? Silver? Where?

(*The* LION *and* SCARECROW *cross* D.S. *on either side of* GATE-KEEPER, *and grab him. The* TINMAN *also has crossed* D.S. *with axe raised, just in case.*)

LION and SCARECROW. Gotcha!!

GATEKEEPER. (*Screams.*) Oh, damn!! I fall for this every night!

DOROTHY. (*Stepping in to* S.L. *side of* SCARECROW.) We're going in to see the Wiz!

GATEKEEPER. Oh, alright. But I don't wanna be around when you wake him up. And don't you go around touching anything. You look with your eyes and not with your hands.

(GATEKEEPER *continues ad lib babble until he completes his exit* R-2, *after the scrim has flown. The* LION *enters through the gate just prior to its flying, and crosses* S.R. *looking for the* WIZ. *The* SCARECROW *enters second crossing to* S.L., *also looking around.* DOROTHY *and the* TINMAN *enter arm in arm, breaking after entry through the gate, with* DOROTHY *moving up the steps to* R.C., *and* TINMAN *moving to* L.C. *The* GATEKEEPER *enters last, and exits as listed above.*)

ACT TWO

SCENE 5

The throne room of the WIZ, *the next instant.*

The mask is in front of the WIZ *monitor. The room is empty except for the* FOUR FRIENDS.

MUSIC #24B: *ENTRY INTO THRONE ROOM*

(*Nine Chords*)

DOROTHY. (*Crossing up steps, then back to* D.R.C.) Mr. Wiz, we're back!

TINMAN. (*Crossing to* C.) Yeah. Old Evillene has been . . . (*Spins with axe.*) done in!! (SCARECROW *crosses up steps to* U.C.)

LION. (*Crosses to* S.R. *side of* TINMAN.) Would you say the lady was liquidated?

(LION *and* TINMAN *do a hand slap, and the* LION *crosses to* L.C. *The* SCARECROW *crosses down steps to* D.R.C.)

DOROTHY. (*Looks under bridge, and then crosses* D.S. *to* D.R.C.) I wonder where he is?

WIZ. (*Voice offstage. In a disembodied voice surrounds us from everywhere.*) I am everywhere! (*They jump in fright. The* LION *crosses to* DOROTHY.)

TINMAN. (*From* C., *crosses* U.S. *a step.*) Well, we've come back to get what you promised.

WIZ. (*Voice offstage.*) I'm busy . . . (DOROTHY *crosses to steps* S.L.)

SCARECROW. (D.R., *looking around.*) Busy? What kind of stuff is that? (DOROTHY *climbs steps to bridge.*)

TINMAN. (*Crossing* S.R. *to* SCARECROW.) It's a copout!!

LION. (*Backing up toward the engine room door . . . shouts.*) You owe us everything right now . . . (*Quiet . . . an apology.*) Mr. Wiz.

DOROTHY. Mr. Wiz, where are you? (DOROTHY *crosses over bridge toward* U.C.)

WIZ. (*Voice offstage and echo.*) Go away . . . (away . . . away . . . away)

DOROTHY. (*Now at the* S.L. *side of the mask.* TINMAN *crosses* D.R.C. SCARECROW *crosses* C. *to steps.*) Oh, listen, Mr. Wiz, you promised . . .

LION. (*Backing into the engine room door, opens it, revealing cranks, wheels, and flashing lights.*) Hey, you guys! I think I found the engine room. (TINMAN *crosses to the* D.S. *side of* LION. DOROTHY *crosses to* S.R. *side of Mask.*)

WIZ. (*Voice offstage. Urgent.*) Go away!

SCARECROW. (*Quick look to what* LION *is doing, then crosses to* R. *of* C. *on:*) Turn the crank! (*The* LION *does so, and mask begins to jiggle, and shake.*)

WIZ. (*Voice—echo.*) Go away! (away . . . away . . . away . . . away)

SCARECROW. The mask is moving. Turn it some more.

(*The* LION *does so, and finally the mask flies out, revealing an open door to the* WIZ's *bedroom. The* SCARECROW *has moved up the steps to the* S.L. *side of the mask, two steps down from the top.*)

WIZ. (*Voice—echo. As mask jiggles and then flies.*) NO! (no . . . no . . . no . . . no)

(*But it is too late. The* WIZ *is standing there in his pajamas with pink*

*curlers in his hair. He ducks out of sight, and then tries to
weasel out of it.*)

DOROTHY. (S.R. *of* WIZ.) Have you seen Mr. Wiz?

WIZ. Uh . . . no . . . I haven't. As a matter of fact, the Wiz
isn't here right now . . .

(*He brushes past* DOROTHY *toward* D.R., *but the* TINMAN *realizes
who it is and mechanically runs toward* D.R., *heading the* WIZ
off, with axe raised. The LION *crosses in to* L. *of* C., DOROTHY
comes down steps to R. *of* C., *and the* SCARECROW *comes down
steps remaining on the first one, between* DOROTHY *and the*
LION. *The* WIZ, *aware of the approach of the* TINMAN, *retreats
toward* S.L., *and thus into the waiting trap of the others. The*
TINMAN *then continues his pursuit to the* S.R. *side of the* WIZ
who is now enclosed by the FOUR FRIENDS *at* C.)

SCARECROW. Then, who are you?

WIZ. Oh, well . . . I'm . . . um . . .

LION. (*Recognizing him.*) A fake!

TINMAN. A fraud!

SCARECROW. A phony!

DOROTHY. (*One step above him on* S.R. *side.*) And how!

SCARECROW. (*One step above him on* S.L. *side.*) And you look just
like anybody else in the morning!

MUSIC #25:   *"WHO DO YOU THINK YOU ARE?"*

FOUR FRIENDS.

WHO . . . WHO DO YOU THINK YOU ARE?
TELL ME HOW . . . HOW COULD YOU GO SO FAR?
THE SHOW IS OVER, THE CURTAIN IS DOWN
AND YOU'VE GOT TO COME CLEAN.
THE TIME IS NOW, YOU MUST 'FESS UP,
AND SAY WHAT YOU MEAN!

SCARECROW.

BABY YOUR . . . YOUR COME-ON WAS MUCH TOO
    COOL

TINMAN.

TELL ME, WHO . . . WHO DID YOU THINK YOU'D
    FOOL?

ALL.

YOU TURNED US ON, THEN YOU TURNED US OFF

BABY, YOU'RE NOT FOR REAL
  DOROTHY.
WE SEE YOU NOW FOR WHAT YOU ARE
TELL ME, HOW DOES IT FEEL?
  ALL.
HOW DOES IT FEEL?
WHO . . . WHO DO YOU THINK YOU ARE?
WHO TOLD YOU . . . TOLD YOU THAT YOU'RE THE
    STAR?
THE GAME IS OVER, IT'S TIME TO COME THROUGH
WE GOT TO GET OVER
WHAT YOU GONNA DO. TELL ME WHO
WHO DO YOU THINK YOU ARE?
WHO DO YOU THINK YOU ARE?
WHO DO YOU THINK YOU ARE?
WHO DO YOU THINK YOU ARE?
WHO DO YOU THINK YOU ARE?
WHO DO YOU THINK YOU ARE?
WHO DO YOU THINK YOU ARE?
WHO DO YOU THINK YOU ARE?
WHO DO YOU THINK YOU ARE?
WHO DO YOU THINK YOU ARE?

(*At the end of the number, the* WIZ *is* D.R., *and the* FOUR FRIENDS
    are. in order to his S.L. *side,* DOROTHY, TINMAN, LION, *and*
    SCARECROW, *with* SCARECROW *at approximately* C.)

WIZ. (*Gets up on his knees.*) Who do I think I am? (*Friends turn
to* S.L.) Who is the Great . . . the Terrible . . . the Omnipotent
Wizard of Oz in reality? (*He gets up . . . pause.*)

TINMAN. Yeah?

WIZ. (*Crossing* D.R. *away from them.*) Just a former nobody from
Omaha, Nebraska.

DOROTHY. (*Crossing to him.*) Nebraska? Why, that's near
Kansas!

WIZ. (*Crossing in to* DOROTHY.) Yeah. It's right next door.
(DOROTHY *crosses to between* SCARECROW *and* LION.)

SCARECROW. (*Crosses* D.S. *a step.*) I don't understand . . .

WIZ. (*From* D.R.C.) Of course not. *Nobody* knows my secret.
(*Crosses in.*) Just as nobody . . . (*Crosses* D.R.) until now
. . . ever sees the real me. Look, y'all . . . (*Crosses in to them.*)
all I ever wanted were the simple things in life . . . (*Crosses* D.S.

of them on the following.) power . . . prestige . . . and money. (*Now* D.L.C., *turns back to them.*) I tried everything back in Omaha. (*Crosses* D.S. *of them to* D.R.) I sold used cars . . . I was a pitchman in a carnival . . . I even peddled bleaching creams from door to door, (*Now* D.R.) but nothing ever worked. (*Crossing to* D.C.) And then, one day, I got the call.

TINMAN. (*A step* D.S. *to* WIZ'S R.) The call?

SCARECROW. (*A step* D.S. *to* WIZ'S L.) The call from who?

WIZ. The call from the Almighty Himself. And that voice said to me: "Son, what you ought to do is spread the Good Word." And I said: "Why?" And the voice said: "For the simple things in life . . . power . . . prestige . . . and money." (*With this, the* WIZ *tries to break to* D.R., *but the* TINMAN'S *axe comes up across his middle, barring his path.*)

TINMAN. Some Almighty voice actually said that to you? (DOROTHY *crosses in to* S.L. *side of* WIZ *through:*)

WIZ. Well, I can't swear whether that message was coming to me live or on tape, but I heard it clear as a bell.

DOROTHY. (*Who has crossed back to between the* LION *and* SCARECROW.) Then what happened?

WIZ. Well, the very next day, I read where . . . (*Brings hands together.*) five thousand folks were gonna get together at a county fair.

TINMAN. Yeah?

WIZ. (*Crossing to* D.R.) So I rented myself a hot air balloon.

LION. Why? (DOROTHY *leans on* LION, SCARECROW *puts his arm on* DOROTHY'S *shoulder.*)

WIZ. Check this out! I come floating down out of the clouds. I lay my maiden message on the multitude, and I whip up the grand-daddy of all revival meetings. Now, unfortunately as my balloon was comin' in low from over the carousel, from out of nowhere, a violent wind . . . (*Spins.*) storm came up . . . and the . . . next . . . thing . . . I . . . knew (*Each word as a beat, and the* FOUR FRIENDS *lean in on four counts. Then, the* WIZ *looks front on one count, and in turn, on the next four beats, the* TINMAN, LION, DOROTHY, *and* SCARECROW *look* D.S.) . . . I was drifting over this huge desert someplace. Then, through an opening in the clouds, I floated down and landed right here in Oz, right in the middle of a ladies' social!

LION. (*Crosses* D.S. *a step.*) Come-come-come, Mr. Wiz, what happened next, my man?

WIZ. (*Crossing to* LION, *hooking his left arm in the* LION'S *right.*)

Well, these ladies had never seen a balloon before. (WIZ *and* LION *cross* S.L. *to* L.C.) They thought a miracle had delivered me to them. And before you could say "wizard" . . . (*He now includes all the* FRIENDS *in his tale.*) they promoted me all over town, and sold tickets for a benefit, at which they said I was going to perform *another* miracle. (*Then, proudly.*) Naturally, I did! (SCARECROW, DOROTHY, *and* TINMAN *have crossed in.*)

LION. Well, yeah. But what kind of another miracle did you put on them cats and kittens?

WIZ. Ahhh . . . (*Starting to speak, suddenly is quiet, looks off* S.L., U.S. *of* LION, *who turns and also looks off* S.L., *to see if anyone is listening.* WIZ *then does the same toward* S.R., *and finding they are alone, beckons with his head for the* TINMAN, DOROTHY, *and* SCARECROW *to move in closer. They do.*) Green glasses! (*The* WIZ *snaps fingers on both hands, and breaks toward* S.R., *doing an exaggerated walk.*)

SCARECROW. (*After the* WIZ *has cleared to* R. *of* C., *steps* D.S.) Say what? (*They don't get it.*)

WIZ. The glasses with the green lenses. (*They still don't see, so he crosses in to make the next point.*) Like the ones everyone's wearing. Just like the pair I was wearing when I landed here. (WIZ *crosses* U.S. *and up the stairs to the second from the top. The* TINMAN *and* SCARECROW, *in utter bewilderment, cross* S.R. *to* R.C., *clearing* WIZ.)

LION. Yeah. But wait a minute, Mr. Wiz, there ain't no big miracle about a pair of green shades . . . (*Said to* DOROTHY *who is still* S.R. *of* LION, *and* S.L. *of the sightlines to the* WIZ.) is there?

MUSIC #26:   *"BELIEVE IN YOURSELF"*

WIZ. The miracle, my friend, is what you allow your eyes to see through them . . . (DOROTHY *and* LION *cross* U.S. *to the* S.L. *side of the* WIZ, *who is now on the first step. They remain on the deck level. In a corresponding move, the* SCARECROW *and* TINMAN *cross* U.S. *to the* S.R. *side of the* WIZ, *with the* TINMAN *closer. The* WIZ *sings to* DOROTHY.)

IF YOU BELIEVE
   (*Front.*)
WITHIN YOUR HEART YOU'LL KNOW
   (*To* SCARECROW.)
THAT NO ONE CAN CHANGE

(WIZ *steps* D.S. *one step.*)
THE PATH THAT YOU MUST GO

BELIEVE WHAT YOU FEEL
    (*To* DOROTHY *and* LION.)
AND KNOW YOU'RE RIGHT BECAUSE
    (*Front.*)
THE TIME WILL COME AROUND
    (*To* SCARECROW *and* TINMAN.)
WHEN YOU'LL SAY IT'S YOURS

[*The* FOUR FRIENDS *sit, with* DOROTHY *on the second step,* S.L. *of*
   C., *and the* LION *at her feet slightly* O.S. *of her. The* TINMAN *is*
   also on the second step, S.R. *of* C., *and the* SCARECROW *is at his*
   feet, seated on the deck, slightly O.S. *of him. The* WIZ *con-*
   tinues, crossing D.C.)

BELIEVE THERE'S A REASON TO BE
BELIEVE YOU CAN MAKE TIME STAND STILL
    (*Crossing to* R.C.)
AND KNOW FROM THE MOMENT YOU TRY
IF YOU BELIEVE, I WILL YOU WILL.

BELIEVE IN YOURSELF
    (*Crosses toward* S.L. *portal.*)
RIGHT FROM THE START
AND YOU WILL HAVE BRAINS
AND YOU'LL HAVE A HEART

AND YOU WILL HAVE COURAGE
    (*Arrives at portal on "courage."*)
TO LAST YOUR WHOLE LIFE THROUGH
    (WIZ *now turns out toward house.*)
IF YOU BELIEVE IN YOURSELF
IF YOU BELIEVE IN YOURSELF
IF YOU BELIEVE IN YOURSELF
MAYPE YOU CAN BELIEVE IN ME, TOO!
    (WIZ *then crosses to* C. *toward* SCARECROW. *The* FRIENDS *all*
   rise.)

Now, then, you *do* believe you have a brain, don't you?

SCARECROW. (*Crosses* D.S. *of* TINMAN *to face* WIZ.) Well, I'd feel a whole lot better if I knew I had something upstairs besides a bunch of straw.

WIZ. All right! If I found green glasses for all of them out there, maybe I can find a brain somewhere in here for you.

(*On this line, the* WIZ *crosses up the steps to a box in the floor of the top platform. He opens a trap door lid where items are kept. As he moves, the* SCARECROW *sits* C. *of the steps, awaiting the presentation of his brain.* DOROTHY *backs up toward* S.L. *to clear and watch.* TINMAN *does the same on the* S.R. *side. The* LION *crosses to the* S.R. *side of the* TINMAN.)

MUSIC: *JAZZ AD LIB UNDERSCORING*

WIZ. (*Fishing into the box, he produces a large spangled box marked "All-Bran."*) Look what we got here. "All-Brain"! Through the miracle of modern science, they have dehydrated, prefrozen, and packaged a distillation of some of the best brains in the world. We're gonna restuff your head with this!

(*The* SCARECROW *is really scared. This may be like a frontal lobotomy. He shakes, and grits his teeth in anticipation of pain. The* WIZ *pours the "All-Brain" which is really glitter, onto the* SCARECROW, *who whirls his head four times, primarily to clear the excess glitter, and then rises, with a big grin, totally changed and refined, the epitome of self-assurance.*)

SCARECROW. Well, *finally* I know where my head is at!

(*Very grandly, and on toe, he crosses to* DOROTHY D.L., *picks her up, whirling her around, then puts her down, big hug, shares the moment of victory with the woman who made it possible.*)

WIZ. (*To* TINMAN.) A heart, you say?

(TINMAN *crosses in to* D.S. *of steps, slightly* S.R. *of* C. *The* LION *crosses to* S.R., *then up the* S.R. *steps to the* R.C. *section of the top platform.*)

TINMAN. Yes!
WIZ. Then a heart it shall be. (*The* WIZ *returns the "All-Bran"*

box to the trap, and produces a large red, satin heart, with the word
"love" across the front. He hides it behind his back as he comes
down the steps to the S.L. *side of the* TINMAN.) You know,
once . . .

TINMAN. Yes?

WIZ. A beautiful young lady gave her heart to me, and now I give
it to you.

(*The* LION *now crosses to the* S.R. *side of the* U.C. *platform, and the*
WIZ *hooks the heart onto the* TINMAN's *chest. The* TINMAN
laughs with glee, as the WIZ *takes one step back up the stairs*
toward U.C. *As he does, the* TINMAN *reaches out, grasping his*
arm, and asks:)

TINMAN. Are the batteries included?

WIZ. At no extra charge! (TINMAN *releases his arm, and the* WIZ
continues back U.C., *turns and watches the* TINMAN.)

TINMAN. (*Realizes it has finally happened, crosses* D.S. *to* D.C.,
poses with axe blade on deck, handle in his right hand.) All you fine
ladies out there . . . ha ha ha . . . (*He kicks the axe blade with*
his right foot, sending it up to land on his right shoulder.) Watch
out! (*He now crosses to* D.R., *and as he turns back in, the*
SCARECROW *runs from* D.L. *where he has watched the proceedings*
with DOROTHY, *and comes to his* FRIEND *to congratulate him. The*
SCARECROW *ends up on the* S.R. *side of the* TINMAN.)

WIZ. (*Turning to* LION *immediately* S.R. *of him.*) As for you,
Jack . . . I bet a couple of totes of the Emerald City courage potion
will do the trick. (*He produces a chalice out of the trap box, sets it*
down, and then pulls out a huge whiskey bottle marked "O&Z," and
pours some into the chalice. Then he pulls out a seltzer bottle, and
gives the mixture a squirt, and it foams up. [Warm water and dry
ice.] As the WIZ *has been concocting the mixture, the* LION *crosses*
down the steps to the deck level. The WIZ *sets all the bottles back*
into the trap, then picks up the chalice, crosses down the steps to
D.C., *and sets it down. He backs up to level the* LION, *slaps him on*
the back and orders: . . .) Drink!

(*The* LION *falls to his knees . . . He wishes Momma was here to*
see him get his courage. The FOUR FRIENDS *close in, anxious for*
his gift to be received, and they encourage his drinking. Finally,
with great trepidation: . . .)

LION. Alright . . . alright . . . (*He gets his snoot down into the chalice . . . the smoke foams up . . . we hear snorting as he drinks . . . The* WIZ *picks up the* LION's *tail, and moving to* U.L. *of the* LION, he places the tip under his foot, and with full force, slams his foot down on the deck, with the end of the tail still under it. The LION *roars in pain, leaps up on his feet. With the first roar, the* WIZ *moves very quickly up on the steps and sits on the third step, facing* S.R. . . . *the picture of innocence. Advancing on the* WIZ, *really going to belt him.*) Alright! (*Sees the* WIZ *has been driven off, and is in a submissive position, he realizes it must be . . . To* DOROTHY, S.L. *of him.*) Alright?

DOROTHY. Alright!

LION. (*To* TINMAN *and* SCARECROW.) Alright?

TINMAN and SCARECROW. Alright!!

LION. (*Getting it together, nothing more to prove, very underplayed.*) Alright!!

(DOROTHY *runs to* LION, *as he joins* TINMAN *and* SCARECROW, *complete rejoicing as all her men have gotten their gifts.*)

DOROTHY. (*Turning away from* FRIENDS, *faces the* WIZ *and crosses in.*) Now it's my turn, Mr. Wiz. Whatcha got in there to get me all the way back home to Kansas?

WIZ. (*Crosses* D.S. *to get chalice* . . .) Dorothy . . . (*Picks up chalice, now* WIZ *and* DOROTHY *have what amounts to a footrace to get back* U.S. *to the trap-box keeping himself between* DOROTHY *and the box.*) I'm sorry. I can do a lot of things for a lot of people, but I just don't know how to get you back home to Kansas. The answer's just not in this box.

(DOROTHY *heartbroken, runs* D.S. *and buries herself in the* TINMAN's *embrace. The* LION *is* U.S. *of them, and he may have to do a number on the* WIZ, *and he's ready. However, the* SCARECROW, *who is* D.R.C., *turns out, pondering, and finally we see his face brighten and he says grandly: . . .*)

SCARECROW. Of course not. (*He sweeps the audience in gesture.*) It's out there somewhere. (*The* WIZ *puts the chalice back in the trap.*)

LION. (*Irritated.*) Out where?

SCARECROW. (*Crossing toward the steps, but remaining on the deck level*, R.C. [*English accent*].) Tell me, my good fellow, do you still have that balloon that brought you here from Kansas?

WIZ. (*Proud to be asked, he comes down the steps, takes the* SCARECROW's *left arm, and the cross* D.C.) Yes, I do. The ladies put it up in the park and made a National Shrine out of it.

SCARECROW. (S.R. *side of* WIZ.) Just as I thought. Now, if that balloon brought you here from Nebraska . . .

WIZ. Uh huh . . .

SCARECROW. Why couldn't it take Dorothea back to Kansas?

WIZ. (*Brightly*.) Why, it certainly could. But first of all . . .

DOROTHY. (*Running eagerly to the* S.L.S.L. *side of the* WIZ, *with the* LION *following to* U.S. *of* WIZ *and* DOROTHY, *and the* TINMAN *to the* S.R. *side of the* SCARECROW.) Yeah! When do we go?

WIZ. (*A sudden thought*.) Now, hold on! There is no way you're gonna get me to leave all this!

DOROTHY. All what?

WIZ. All my power, my prestige, and my money! (*He crosses to* D.R.)

DOROTHY. (*Following him, real bite*.) You mean your big old empty room, where nobody comes to see you, and you're *afraid* to go out, 'less people find out you're foolin' them.

WIZ. (*Whirling on her, and backing her to* R. *of* C., *where* SCARECROW *takes her shoulders. Yells:*) I am NOT afraid!! (*As he reaches the group, the* TINMAN's *axe comes up, barring his way, and the* LION *growls, and means it. The* WIZ *has second thoughts*.) I just keep a low profile.

DOROTHY. (*Moves to* WIZ.) You know . . . (*She grabs his left arm*.) I bet if you got started all over again someplace . . .

WIZ. (*Crossing toward* D.R., DOROTHY *pursues and holds his arm*.) Oh, no . . . no . . .

DOROTHY. You could do all this . . . and even have some friends.

WIZ. (*Turning to her*.) Friends? Do you really think so? (*Starts to turn away* S.R.)

DOROTHY. (*Grabbing his other hand, turning* WIZ *back to her*.) Aw, you're not so bad . . . once a person gets to know you. (*The same magic that helped the* LION *in* "BE A LION.")

WIZ. (*Mulling it over. Are "Friends" enough? He breaks* R., *to exit and go to his bedroom to cry alone*.) Friends, huh?

DOROTHY. (*Crosses two steps* S.L., *teasing*.) And when we get back to Kansas, I'll give you my silver slippers.

WIZ. Well, what are we waiting for? (*He exits* R-1.)

MUSIC #27: *"HOME"*
(Dance.)

ACT TWO

SCENE 6

The balloon site in Emerald City.

On the WIZ's *exit, the* FOUR FRIENDS *move up the steps to the top of the platform.* DOROTHY *is* R. *of* C., LION L. *of her,* SCARECROW L. *of* LION, TINMAN L. *of* SCARECROW.

The People of Emerald City arrive, entering from L-1. *The Ladies have nests of balloons for farewell gifts. They circle* D.S. *of the platforms, and go up the* S.R. *stairs to the top, giving the balloons to* DOROTHY *as they pass her.*

The orchestra plays two choruses of "HOME." *Behind the* FRIENDS, *the Wiz Monitor flies out, and during the second chorus, the balloon which brought the* WIZ *from Nebraska flies in.*

At the end of the second chorus, the Lady closest to D.R. *sees the* WIZ *coming, and faints into the arms of her Gentleman.*

The WIZ *enters* D.R., *in white flight helmet, goggles, jump uit, high boots, and long white cape with green lining. He circles across to* D.L., *then up the stairs to* U.C.

The FRIENDS *cross down off the platform and join the crowd facing the* WIZ.

WIZ. (*Helmet off, flings into balloon.*) My fellow Ozians. . .(*They start to bow.*) No . . . uh uh. Just let me say . . .my friends. (WIZ *puts on over-sized green glasses.* CITIZENS *cheer.* WIZ *cuts them off with a gesture.*) On this memorable day when friends . . . (WIZ *pulls them in.*) must part . . . (WIZ *parts hands and they move back to two groups,* S.R. *and* S.L.) Remember, to every thang . . . (WIZ *to* R.C. *on top platform.*) there is a season. (WIZ *back to* U.C.) And remember there is a time to keep. . . (WIZ's *and* CITIZENS' *hands up*.) and a time to cast away. (*All put hands down*.)

CITIZENS. Well . . .

WIZ. Yes, I said a time to keep . . . (*All hands up*.) and a time to cast away. (*All hands down*.)

CITIZENS. Well . . .

WIZ. And today is both times for us. (WIZ *conducts* S.L. *group*.)

STAGE LEFT CITIZENS. Well????? (WIZ *conducts* S.R. *group*.)

STAGE RIGHT CITIZENS. Well!!!!

WIZ. I said a time to keep . . .

CITIZENS. Uh!!   NO!

WIZ. I said a time to keep . . .

CITIZENS: Uh!!   lunge

WIZ. And a time to remember.

CITIZENS. Uh!!   mmhm

WIZ. Yes, I said a time to remember.

CITIZENS. Uh!!   lunge

WIZ. And at this very . . .

CITIZENS. Uh!

WIZ. . . . same . . .

CITIZENS. Uh!

WIZ. . . . moment . . .

CITIZENS. Uh!

WIZ. . . . a time . . . (*Elongated word*. CITIZENS *all cheer. After a couple of beats*, WIZ *cuts them off*.) when we must . . .

CITIZENS. What must we do? (WIZ *takes off his glasses during this line*.)

WIZ. Cast away. (*He tosses his glasses on "cast," toward the* S.R. *group, where they are caught by one man*. CITIZENS *break loose in wild cheering as the* WIZ *crosses* D.S. *to* D.C. WIZ, *over their chatter*.) A time when we must stop . . . (*Silence*.) holding on to the things that make us feel safe!

CITIZENS. Yes! (*All put hands up*.)

WIZ. And embrace what we fear. (*All put hands down slowly*.) Ourselves in all our beautiful hang-ups!! (CITIZENS *applaud, agreeing with* WIZ, *and closing in on him*. WIZ *kneels on one knee* D.C., *and holds his right hand up . . . immediate silence and attention*.) we have got to know in our hearts . . . (*Indicates heart*.) that the things that we hold up as sacred, are sometimes holding us d-d-d-down!! (WIZ *rises and crosses* D.R., CITIZENS *kneel facing him*.) Down! When you know you ought to be up! (WIZ *kneels* D.R.)

Down! (CITIZENS *up*.) Afraid to wade through strange and turbulent waters. (WIZ *makes gestures of waves*, CITIZENS *follow, undulating*.) Down!! (CITIZENS *kneel*, WIZ *up, crossing* S.L. *among them*.) Burning in the heat of your own lies . . . (WIZ *at* C. *by here*.) when you ought to be reaching up . . . (WIZ *crossing toward* D.L.) up . . . up! (CITIZENS *rise and follow* WIZ *toward* D.L., *cheering*. WIZ *holds up hand for silence*.) To touch the frozen fingers of truth. (WIZ *Crosses* D.S. *of* CITIZENS *toward* D.R.C.) You . . . have got to peel off all your clothes to find out who you truly are! . . . Y'all gonna do it? (CITIZENS, *shocked at such a suggestion, turn* U.S. *in stony silence*.) Shall I do it?

CITIZENS. (*Turning* D.S. *to* WIZ.) Yes!

WIZ. (*Takes off his cape, tosses it to a man* S.R. *of him*.) Ooooo! I have done it! (*Crosses* D.C.) I have stepped outside of myself.

CITIZENS. Step!

WIZ. In order to dig inside my own soul.

CITIZENS. Step!

WIZ. In order to see . . . what I ought to have seen . . . before.

CITIZENS. Step! Step!

WIZ. Now you have got to do it! (CITIZENS *all cheer, and express an orgy of delight. After a few beats of observation,* WIZ *leaps in the air, a grand gesture, and* CITIZENS *all fall silent. The* WIZ *turns* D.S.) It is not enough to know where you're going. You also have to know where you're coming from. Y'all got it?

CITIZENS. Got it!!

MUSIC #28: *"Y'ALL GOT IT?"*

WIZ.
I GOT TO LEAVE, SO I'VE PACKED MY BAG AND I'M GOING
    (*Crosses* D.R.)
I'VE GOT A DATE, SO DON'T ASK ME TO STAY
    (*Crosses* D.L.)
'CAUSE I'M SHOWING

YOU WERE ALWAYS READY FOR NEW WIZARDRY
YOU MUST HAVE THOUGHT MIRACLES COME EASY TO ME
TAKE WHAT I GAVE YOU AND PUT IT UP ON A SHELF

'CAUSE NOW IT'S TIME FOR THIS HERE WIZ
TO WIZ ON HIMSELF
AND I'M WIZIN'
    (*Crosses up* S.R. *steps to* U.C.)

GIVE ME A REASON WHY I SHOULD STAY
AND I'LL JUDGE IT
MY MIND IS MADE UP, SO NOTHIN' YOU SAYS
GONNA BUDGE IT
Y'ALL COPPED A WHOLE LOT OF MAGIC FROM ME
BUT THIS, THE GREATEST MAGIC
THAT YOU'LL EVER SEE
IF YOU BLINK MORE THAN ONE TIME,
THE KID WILL BE GONE.
AND YOU WILL HAVE TO HOOK UP
THE REST ON YOUR OWN
AND DO YOU KNOW WHAT I THINK ABOUT THAT?
    (WIZ *crosses* U.S. *of* DOROTHY *to* D.L.)
YOUR WORK'S CUT OUT FOR YOU,
SO IT'S NOT ABOUT IFS, BUTS OR ANDS
'CAUSE WHEN I LEAVE THIS TOWN
I'M LEAVING IT ALL IN YOUR HANDS
I PACKED UP MY CLOTHES AND
I PACKED UP MY POWER.
I'M LEAVING THIS PLACE
IN LESS THAN ONE HALF AN HOUR
IF YOU'LL LOOK UP IN THE SKY,
YOU'LL KNOW JUST WHO IT IS,
IT'S NOT A BIRD OR A PLANE
IT'S JUST THE LITTLE OLE WIZ
AND GUESS WHO'S ON AFTER THAT?
    (*Dance section.*)
GIVE ME A REASON WHY I SHOULD STAY
AND I'LL JUDGE IT
MY MIND IS MADE UP SO NOTHING YOU SAY'S
GONNA BUDGE IT
I PACKED UP MY CLOTHES
AND I PACKED UP MY POWER
I'M LEAVING THIS PLACE
IN LESS THAN ONE HALF AN HOUR
IF YOU LOOK UP IN THE SKY
YOU'LL KNOW JUST WHO IT IS

NOT A BIRD OR A PLANE
JUST THE LITTLE OLE WIZ
AND GUESS WHO'S ON AFTER THAT?
  CITIZENS.
Y'ALL GOT IT
Y'ALL GOT IT
Y'ALL GOT IT
  WIZ.
TALKIN' 'BOUT LEAVIN' HERE
  CITIZENS.
Y'ALL GOT IT
Y'ALL GOT IT
Y'ALL GOT IT
  WIZ.
TALKIN' 'BOUT LEAVIN' HERE
  CITIZENS.
Y'ALL GOT IT
Y'ALL GOT IT
Y'ALL GOT IT
  WIZ.
Y'ALL GOT IT?

Come on, Dorothy, it's time to leave. (*He crosses* U.S. *to the balloon, gets in it, and it immediately flies away. The* CITIZENS *exit* S.R. *and* S.L.)
  TINMAN. Dorothy, the balloon . . .
  SCARECROW. (*From* U.C.) Dorothy! Dorothy!
DOROTHY. (*As she runs* U.C. *trying to catch the balloon.*) Mr. Wiz . . . Mr.Wiz . . .

ACT TWO

SCENE 7

Somewhere else in Oz. The next instant.

As the balloon disappears, the pieces of Emerald City also fly out or slide out either side of the stage, so that all that remains are the C. *section of steps.*

Despite the fact that DOROTHY *still has her* FOUR FRIENDS, *she throws a tantrum at her disappointment. She pulls the ribbons from her hair, stamps her feet.*

DOROTHY. Mr. Wiz! You left me. Now I'll bet I'll never get home to Kansas. Never.

MUSIC #28A   *ADDAPERLE'S ENTRANCE*

(There is a puff of smoke from the R-1 *entrance, and as it clears, we see* ADDAPERLE, *dazed and confused as usual.)*

ADDAPERLE. (*At* D.R.C.) Where am I?

DOROTHY. (*From* L.C. *she runs to* ADDAPERLE.) Addaperle!

ADDAPERLE. Dorothy! Dorothy, baby! (*They hug each other, with* ADDAPERLE'S *head on the* D.S. *side. She sees others standing* C., *breaks the embrace, and steps back a step.*) How come you joined the circus, child?

DOROTHY. No. They're my friends. They came with me to see the Wiz, too.

ADDAPERLE. (*A step back in to* DOROTHY.) Oh, you saw him.

DOROTHY. Yeah.

ADDAPERLE. And you got what you wanted?

DOROTHY. Well, *they* did. But I still haven't gotten home to Kansas, yet.

ADDAPERLE. Oh. I thought maybe *this* was Kansas.

DOROTHY. No.

ADDAPERLE. Well, listen. Now, how about Glinda? She ought to be able to think of something.

DOROTHY. Who?

ADDAPERLE. (*Annoyed that* DOROTHY *hasn't remembered such an important person.*) I told you about my sister, Glinda. The Good Witch of the South. (LION, TINMAN, *and* SCARECROW *cross* R. *to* DOROTHY.) She's the prettiest of all us witches. Takes after me.

TINMAN. (*Between the* LION *and the* SCARECROW.) Where can we find her?

ADDAPERLE. Oh, don't worry. I'll bring Glinda here before you can say "Great Googamooga Suger Booga." Just a wave of my magic hankie . . . (*She waves it and to her surprise, magic does happen.*)

MAGIC #29: "A RESTED BODY"

(*An unfolding tent unit comes on from the* L-3 *entrance, rolls to* U.C., *about the steps and opens. With it come the* QUADLINGS, *who are in* GLINDA's *domain.*) Listen!! That's Glinda. That's Glinda's theme song. (*Noticing the* QUADLINGS.) Look at 'em. They're coming out of the woodwork. Go ahead, Glinda. Work your show, baby.

(ADDAPERLE *and the* FOUR FRIENDS *move to* R.C. DOROTHY *and the* SCARECROW *sit on the ground.* ADDAPERLE, TINMAN, *and* LION *stand* U.S. *of them. The tent opens, and* GLINDA, *The Good Witch of the South, appears, and indeed is the prettiest of all the Witches. She is also wise in the ways of show-business, as her song will indicate.*)

GLINDA.
COME OVER HERE AND REST A WHILE
LOOK AT THE TRIP YOU'VE MADE
I KNOW YOU MUST BE TIRED BY NOW
SO REST HERE IN THE SHADE
    (GLINDA *and* ESCORTS *cross* D.C.)
OH, THE JOURNEY THAT YOU HAD TO MAKE
I'VE WATCHED YOU BEAR THE LOAD
BUT YOU CAN ALWAYS STAY AT MY PLACE
WHEN YOU COME OFF THE ROAD
    (*Now at* D.C.)
AND IF YOU EVER NEED SOMEONE
COUNT ON ME ANYTIME
    (*Horizontal lift.*)
I'LL BE HERE TO LAY YOU DOWN
BECAUSE A RESTED BODY IS A RESTED MIND
BECAUSE A RESTED BODY IS A RESTED MIND
    (*On "mind,"* GLINDA's GIRLS *sit.*)

A RESTED BODY IS A RESTED MIND
    (*At the end of the number, with an* ESCORT *on each arm,* GLINDA *crosses* D.L.)

ADDAPERLE. (*From* R.C.) Glinda! Glinda! Glinda, it's me. Addaperle! (ADDAPERLE *crosses in to* C.)
GLINDA. (*Does big take, and all the sophistication drops away, as she crosses in, and gets real "down home."*) Addaperle!! (*Three sets of finger kisses.*)

ADDAPERLE. You sure know how to get down.

GLINDA. Well, it may be so, but it's costing me a fortune to do it.
Now come over here, Darlin' . . . (*On last line,* GLINDA *takes*
ADDAPERLE *toward* D.L. *to meet some of her friends.* GLINDA *is* U.S.
of ADDAPERLE. DOROTHY *runs after* GLINDA *and pulling her away
from* ADDAPERLE:)

DOROTHY. Miss Glinda! My name's Dorothy . . . (*Pulls*
GLINDA *toward* R.C.) and these are my friends . . .

GLINDA. (*Breaks away* S.L. *to* L. *of* C.) I know all about you.

DOROTHY. You do?

GLINDA. Oh, I been watchin' you on my crystal ball, hoppin'
around from one witch to another . . . hittin' 'em with houses, and
washin' 'em down the drain . . .

DOROTHY. (*A step* S.R. *to* D.S. *of* LION.) Yeah. Nobody knows the
trouble I've seen.

GLINDA. Well, relax, child. (GLINDA *crosses* U.S. *of* DOROTHY,
and around her to the S.R. *side. In passing, she chucks the* LION
under the chin and says . . .) Hi, Pussycat!! (*Big grin from* LION.)

DOROTHY. Then you'll help me get home again?

GLINDA. Why, honey, you got your silver slippers. They'll take
you home in no time. Don't you ever talk to your feet?

(*During the last three lines,* ADDAPERLE *has singled out one of*
    GLINDA's ESCORTS, *and is inspecting him, noting a perfect
    body, well-groomed mustache and beard.*)

DOROTHY. No . . .

MUSIC #30: *"BELIEVE IN YOURSELF"*

GLINDA. Well, Addaperle . . . Addaperle . . . (*Sees what*
ADDAPERLE *is up to, a mild reprimand.*) Addaperle! (ADDAPERLE
stops the flirting, pays attention to GLINDA . . . *little embarrassed
laugh.*) You could have told her the secret right off!

ADDAPERLE. (*Crossing* D.S.) Well, of course I could have. But
look at all the people I'd have put out of work.

DOROTHY. Miss Glinda, please tell me the secret.

GLINDA.
BELIEVE WHAT YOU FEEL AND KNOW YOU'RE RIGHT
BECAUSE THE TIME WILL COME AROUND
WHEN YOU SAY IT'S YOURS
    (*Crosses with* DOROTHY *to* D.L.C.)

BELIEVE THAT YOU CAN GO HOME
BELIEVE YOU CAN FLOAT ON AIR
THEN CLICK YOUR HEELS THREE TIMES
    (*She pushes* DOROTHY *to* D.L.)
IF YOU BELIEVE, THEN YOU'LL BE THERE

BELIEVE IN YOURSELF, RIGHT FROM THE START
    (*The unit folds up, and the two side tents are returned to their*
    boxes.)
BELIEVE IN THE MAGIC THAT'S INSIDE YOUR HEART
BELIEVE WHAT YOU SEE
NOT WHAT LIFE TOLD YOU TO

BUT BELIEVE IN YOURSELF
IF YOU BELIEVE IN YOURSELF
JUST BELIEVE IN YOURSELF
AS I BELIEVE IN YOU
    (*On last* "*you,*" GLINDA *is lifted by three of her* ESCORTS.
    Then, ADDAPERLE, *who has been* U.S. *of* GLINDA *and*
    DOROTHY, *is lifted horizontally, by four of* GLINDA'S MEN.)

C'mon, Addaperle . . . We got a lot of catching up to do. (GLINDA
is carried off L-1.)
    ADDAPERLE. (*As she is also carried off* L-1.) What a way to go,
baby!!
    DOROTHY. 'Bye, Addaperle.
    ADDAPERLE. 'Bye, Dorothy.

(*The* QUADLINGS *also exit* L-1. *The* TINMAN, *flanked by the*
    SCARECROW *to his* S.R. *side, and the* LION *to his* S.L. *side,*
    follows to R.C.)

DOROTHY. (*Turns to them.*) You mean, that's all there ever was to
it? Just clickin' my heels three times, and I'm home?
    LION. Ain't that something, Little Momma. I guess it's about time
to go home, huh? (DOROTHY *crosses to* LION, *and they hug.*)
    SCARECROW. Just think, you coulda gone back before you even
met me. (*The thought suddenly sobers him.*)
    TINMAN. Yeah. Before you even got tied up with any of us. (*A*
step in.) Honey, what a shame. (*A moment of silence. Then*
DOROTHY *crosses in to* TINMAN.)

DOROTHY. No! It wasn't a shame. 'Cause if I'd gone back then, I never would have known if you got your heart . . . (DOROTHY *crosses to* SCARECROW, D.S. *of him to his* S.R. *side, where she faces him.*) and I'd never have seen you get your brains . . . (*She starts back to the* LION, *who turns away to* D.S.; *she can't hold back the tears any longer for he has been her dearest friend of all.*) and you . . . you . . . (*She collapses in his arms.*)

MUSIC #31: *"HOME"*

(*The* LION *holds her fraternally for a moment, and then fully, as he turns her so that she is on the* S.L. *side of the group. The* LION, *too, is close to tears.*)

LION. Dorothy . . . (*He breaks the embrace, and gets control of his feelings.*) do you really have to go?

SCARECROW. (*Trying to remain objective, fighting back tears.*) Well, logically, even if she did go . . . (*He now turns to* DOROTHY.) if you kept the silver slippers, you could come back any time you wanted to!

DOROTHY. (*She crosses to him, taking his right hand.*) And I will, Scarecrow . . . I *promise* I'll come back . . . (*She moves* D.S. *of* SCARECROW *still holding his hand.*) but right now, don't you all see . . . (*Releases his hand, and crosses* D.S. *to* D.R.C.)

WHEN I THINK OF HOME, I THINK OF A PLACE
WHERE THERE'S LOVE OVERFLOWING
> (TINMAN *and* SCARECROW *cross to her,* TINMAN *to her right,* SCARECROW *to her left. They each take a hand.*)

, I WISH I WAS BACK THERE
WITH THE THINGS I'VE BEEN KNOWING
WIND THAT MAKES THE TALL GRASS BEND INTO
    LEANING
SUDDENLY THE RAINDROPS THAT FALL HAVE A
    MEANING
SPRINKLING THE SCENE, MAKES IT ALL CLEAN
> On *"Sprinkling,"* the LION *gets down on all fours.*)

MAYBE THERE'S A CHANCE FOR ME TO GO BACK
NOW THAT I HAVE SOME DIRECTION

(DOROTHY *releases* TINMAN'S *and* SCARECROW'S *hands, and crosses* C. *to the* LION *on:*)

IT SURE WOULD BE NICE TO BE BACK HOME
WHERE THERE'S LOVE AND AFFECTION
AND JUST MAYBE I CAN CONVINCE TIME TO SLOW
    UP
GIVING ME ENOUGH TIME IN MY LIFE TO GROW UP
TIME, BE MY FRIEND, LET ME START AGAIN

(*On "Time," the three start a slow exit, fading out of* DOROTHY'S *imagination. The* LION *starts toward* L-2, *pauses, and comes back for one brief moment to press his head against* DOROTHY'S *left thigh. Then he completes his exit, crawling out on all fours toward* L-2. *The* TINMAN *backs slowly out* R-1, *and the* SCARECROW *backs out* R-2)

SUDDENLY, MY WORLD'S GONE AND CHANGED ITS
    FACE
BUT STILL I KNOW WHERE I'M GOING
I HAVE HAD MY MIND SPUN AROUND IN SPACE
AND YET, I'VE WATCHED IT GROWING
AND IF YOU'RE LISTENING, GOD
PLEASE, DON'T MAKE IT HARD
    (*Kneels.*)
TO KNOW IF WE SHOULD BELIEVE THE THINGS WE
    SEE
TELL US, SHOULD WE TRY TO STAY
OR SHOULD WE RUN AWAY
    (*Up.*)
OR IS IT BETTER JUST TO LET THINGS BE?
    (*By now, the* SCARECROW, TINMAN, *and* LION *have disappeared, leaving* DOROTHY *alone for:*)

LIVING HERE IN THIS BRAND NEW WORLD
MIGHT BE A FANTASY,
BUT IT'S TAUGHT ME TO LOVE,
SO IT'S REAL TO ME
AND I LEARNED THAT WE MUST LOOK
INSIDE OUR HEARTS TO FIND
A WORLD FULL OF LOVE

LIKE YOURS, LIKE MINE
LIKE HOME
> (*She clicks her heels three times,* TOTO *comes Onstage from* L-1, *and runs to* C., *where* DOROTHY *sees him and says:*)

Toto!!

CURTAIN

PROPERTY PLOT

free standing clothes line
2 work shirts
1 pair overalls
laundry basket, half filled with clean laundry
1 milk pail
2 weatherbeaten wooden boards approx. 1' x 6'
    (Uncle Henry)
5 rolling stools (Munchkins)
magic bag (Addaperle)
flower trick
slate with white chalk
wand with silks
colored handkerchief trick
6 three foot light canes with multicolored ribbons
    attached one end
4 yellow staffs (Yellow Brick Road)
1 autograph book with pencil (Munchkin)
1 styrofoam axe (Tinman)
1 lace hankie (Lion)
1 oil can (Dorothy)
talcum powder (Poppy)
4 police badges (Mice)
1 police whistle on string (Head Mouse)
1 cigar (Head Mouse)
3 large keys on key ring (Gatekeeper)
4 pairs of green sunglasses (Gatekeeper)
Evillene's rolling throne with 50' of rope
1 bullhorn (Lord High Underling)
1 whip (Lord High Underling)
3 burlap bags (Winkies)
2 water buckets with small amount of glitter (Lion)
4 electric lamps (Winkies)
1 soiled apron (Dorothy)
1 oversize whiskey bottle with the legend: "J.Z."
1 seltzer bottle—practical
1 large goblet
"hot" ice in goblet
1 large valentine heart, trimmed in lace, hookable to Tinman costume

1 oversize cereal box half filled with glitter, with the legend:
    "All Brain"
16 helium filled, green balloons on strings
4 assorted sizes, gift wrapped boxes

ACT ONE

Pre-set On Stage

    clothes line—stage right of center
    2 work shirts—on clothes line
    1 pair of overalls—on clothes line
    laundry basket—downstage of clothes line
    1 milk pail—stage left of center

Stage Right

    1 styrofoam axe
    Evillene's throne with 50' of rope
    1 bullhorn
    1 whip
    2 water buckets with small amount of glitter in each
    soiled apron
    1 Munchkin rolling stool

Stage Left

    2 weatherbeaten boards
    4 Munchkin rolling stools
    Addaperle's magic bag
        In bag: flower trick
                    small slate with chalk
                    wand with silks
                    colored handkerchief trick
    6 three foot light canes with ribbon (set in # portal)
    4 seven foot yellow staffs
    1 autograph book with pencil
    1 lace hanky

1 oil can (set in #1 portal)
talcum powder
4 police badges
1 cigar
1 police whistle on string
3 large keys on key rings
4 pairs of green glasses
3 burlap bags stuffed with paper
4 electric lamps
16 helium filled balloons
4 (assorted sizes) gift wrapped boxes

Present in "Wiz's" Magic Box Built Into Throne Room Platform

1 oversize whiskey bottle
1 large goblet with "hot" ice
1 large valentine heart
cereal box of "All Bran"
1 seltzer bottle

COSTUME LIST

DOROTHY
    same costume throughout—apron for Courtyard, cape for end

ADDAPERLE

SCARECROW
    needs to be torn up in capture

TINMAN
    needs to be damaged in capture (later restored)

LION

WIZ
    3 costumes—as himself on first entrance; pajamas and flying suit
    in Act Two

EVILLENE
    include cape and golden crown (duplicate for Dorothy)

GLINDA

AUNT EM.

UNCLE HENRY.

1 TORNADO

11 WIND DANCERS
    2 with poles

2 PEOPLE IN THE WIND

6 MUNCHKINS
    include castered stools

4 YELLOW BRICK ROAD DANCERS

95

COSTUME LIST

5 Kalidahs
fit together to become one creature

5 Poppies

4 Mice

Gatekeeper

2 Throne Guards

14 Emerald City Citizens

3 Crows

20 Winkies
includes Lord High, Messenger, and fittings for 1 Tourist
Winkie and 1 Medic Winkie

Head Winged Monkey

12 Winged Monkeys

16 Quadlings